PRINTS OF HIS PALM

WITH EVERY TOUCH OF HIS HANDS

LISHON K. JONES

ACKNOWLEDGMENT

In debt, I would like to thank Book Marketers' Project Managers Jack Hudson and Kendrick Lazarus and My editor Anne for believing in my dreams to become a writer and inspiring me daily with reassurance along the way that I can execute this talent seamlessly with confidence. I'd like to thank God for my inner source of strength and inspiration for writing and sharing this unique talent to the world.

I would like to thank my many supporters from Jamaica, United States and Canada for their encouragement to never give up and keep writing. Special thank you to my mom, Angella Clarke, who provided a shoulder to lean on when I felt like giving up; her warmhearted and nurturing attributes ignites my urges to complete my book. My siblings Trisha, Jemoy, Lemar and Audley, was my distraction and comfort through the toughest times, but reassured me that "we are here for you, you can do this!" They made sure my thoughts and mind was free and consumed by their love. The feeling of overcoming this challenge and getting to the finish line is an amazing accomplishment, this happened because you guys held my hands and helped me there. It was worth the journey. Many thanks to you all. I anticipate this walk will be an inspiration, clarification and an addition to the world's collection of love stories.

TABLE OF CONTENTS

THE INTERRUPTED WEDDING

"As we stand here before God to witness the matrimony of Beverly and Thomas, we will now listen to each read their vows, "Bev you go first," Pastor Bishop Slogan dictates.

"You are my world, Thomas; making me happy is all you do, and I'm grateful for that. My body and soul tingle at the sound of your name, and my heart doubles tap when I look at you. I promise to cherish our love and be honest and kind and to never make you sad or blue till death do us part."

"Beverly, you are so beautiful inside out. I'm lucky to have found a rose like you amongst thorns, possessing indescribable values a man yearns for in a woman. You complete me, and I promise to never take our love for granted or even make you cry, but if you do cry, it must be for happiness, and if you are sad, it must be ......"

"No, no, please don't, Thomas - I love you! Please...." a voice yelled from the crowd.

It was a shocking and terrifying moment no one could imagine would have happened. A beautiful day with the wind kissing on our skin and the sun setting beyond the sea, encouraging the photographers and well-wishers to capture the perfect moments for a thousand years.

The crowd, confused, stared back and forth, gossiping with the bride and groom, speechless.

2

This is an embarrassing moment, I thought. I really needed to do something, but what could I do? I stepped forward as she stared at Thomas and asked, "Do you have anything to say?" Thomas looked as puzzled as I am and sighed as if he was being bothered looking at Bev trying to find the right words to say, I presumed.

Bev shook her head, and the pastor asked that the person wait until the moment to object to the Bride and Groom getting married, if they chose to do so, at that time. The crowded area of well-wishers and families was now a courtyard of angry protestors demanding an answer, but instead, the pastor drew their attention back to the bride and groom and reminded them of what they were here to celebrate.

Bev felt betrayed, and suddenly, what was a beautiful bride was now weeping like a widow. She begged the pastor and guest for a moment while she decided what to do and asked that they help themselves to some cocktail in the meantime. She looked at Thomas and ran, devastated and overwhelmed with sadness and embarrassment as a day of joy and happiness was destroyed by a phrase no one will forget.

We've planned this event for months, and he didn't care to share his infidelity, or he's so selfish he wanted to have them both even after making his commitment to Bev? I wanted to cry for her - an embarrassment that could be avoided if it was carefully thought through in order to save money and a soft heart.

Not every moment of a carefully planned event will turn out to be a happy ending, but this special day should be. I wish I could snap my finger and the time-reversed just to save my best friend from a devastated, unscheduled truth. As I walked to the end of the hallway, she was sitting on the grass at the back of the plantation, smothering in her tears.

"I just wanted to be happy; why is this so hard, Liana?" I begged him so much to tell me the truth that we would work it out, and promise me nothing unexpected would spoil our day, whether from his past or current situation. Look at me!" I wanted to believe him so bad that he has changed, but I've learned that no matter what you do, you cannot change the mindset of a person; they will need to develop the courage to do so. How could I be so stupid!"

"I'm sorry, Bev, don't be so hard on yourself words cannot describe how I feel right now, but I'm always here for you no matter what." I hugged her, and before long, Thomas came.

"Bev, I beg you, please, we need to talk," he stuttered.

Without hesitation, she stared at him and said, "This better be good because God knows I can't take it."

I looked at her with curiosity. "Will you be okay?" I asked

"I will Liana, thanks; I'll let you know if I need anything."

I went to a quiet place alone, and my mind ventured peacefully to the day I met James. It's weird how I thought of him in this moment, and Lord knows how special he made me feel!

The moment I saw him I envisioned how my life would be, I imagined it to be exotic, fun, most memorable and includes great sex. The surprises I thought about were gushing through my brain as I wondered how my heart would handle such love, such distraction from my personal life. I would consider myself lucky to have captivated such a man. A man with whom I can live a fun life and be happy. But we all know the life we dream of exists only in fairy tales or just in our dreams. We would need more than just a few words and a handsome man to make a woman of my status give in all her love and dreams, even the fantasies of life, to a man who meets her eyes. We as women, tend to visualize men as supreme beings who always seem to know the right thing to say, the right thing to do, how to make love, and how to keep a woman happy.

I imagined they know it all; but in this life, it doesn't work that way. We need to help our men along the way but is it worth it? Will he feel less of a man if we help him to be more suitable, more sexual, more self-aware, or even how to confidently have a fruitful conversation with our friends and, of course the worst case scenario of finding another version of ourselves after all that alignment. Often times I wonder how a man will react when we take the initiative and provide a lecture to improve on personalities to be more compatible and interactive or his overall life experience, but when this is offered, it is not always accepted - the outcome varies for some but in essence we've heard from our partners' various stories, using a barrier to shield any probability of improvement.

The questions are being asked countless times by our women: how can we make the process seamless, less intimidating, and have our men feel they are enough. The message to our men "You're enough for us, but we have needs, too." we are not asking for perfection or a design being created in a laboratory but at least the basic should be outstanding which can be observed. Often times women are proactive and burden themselves with the task of a man, the responsibilities, ideas and mentorship, it's not to belittle his masculinity but to demonstrate power and protection to show our love and loyalty to him.

It's our job - a full time job to keep him entertained and focus always on us. To make him happy and attend to all his needs. We tend to be submissive when we are treated like "Queens." The consequences are inevitable when we are approached by a man: we make constant eye contact, and we take note of body structure, attire, posture, and smile. The approach is not the answer, but it's a part of the equation - a starting point to something meaningful, something great, and even magical. The conversations are not always our interest but nevertheless we pay attention and share ideas redirecting the topic to where it seems more comfortable for us, which lead to asking the right questions.

Our minds are weapons that defeat our ability to maintain a good conversation. As women, we think too much sometimes; before we are approached, we fill our thoughts with questions surrounding him. We take these on our first date, first kiss, and the bedroom. Instead of paying attention to what is most important on the first date, we hoped that at the end of the evening, we would be kissed or invited home, we fantasized about the lips and how they would feel for the first time - asking ourselves if he's good at it, what's his techniques, will his eyes be closed, does he insert his tongue first, cover our mouth with his or will he be just perfect! The bedroom theories are constantly raving on our minds as we desire the best sensation during intercourse. We draft our predictions by mesmerizing the size of his sexual organ, visualizing how it would feel and how many orgasms we can reach - tempting to ask the duration of each round.

A woman's mind never stops thinking when she lies peacefully with her partner. We anticipate how affectionate and comforting he could be before, during, and after intercourse. We sometimes make preparations for the future when we experience our first sexual intervention with our partner, so we ensure he's properly fed, he's the center of our attention, and meet our friends and family anxious to highlight him on some if not all social media platforms just to show we belong to someone we're taken! We are "First Lady"!

We wear our best undergarments or purchase more to actively ignite his interest; we change our overall appearance at times based on his needs and wants, not limited to his sexual requests and preferences. When we extend our kindness to our lovers, we expect unconditional obvious interest and a constant communication pattern, especially when a mobile connection is required and is not received. The expectation is to respond via text message or phone call. Some men believe that it's best sometimes not to respond to a message or phone call because they may not know what to say, but in our opinion, it's best to reply either saying, "I'll think about it," "I'm not sure," or a simple "okay" leaving an unread message unattended at times creates a negative reaction and insecurity for your partner. This frustration will lead to other abnormalities that were identified initially in the relationship, but many at times, we suddenly use the opportunity to express our opinions, hoping for a positive outcome. In reality, it usually ends with a breakup based on individual expressions, mistrust, miscommunication, and mix-emotions, or the partner simply acknowledges his mistake and apologizes - Oh, I wish this happens a lot, but truth be told, it doesn't! When a man truly loves a woman, they will fight to save their relationship despite the disagreements encountered. In some cases, patience is key; give your partner time to recuperate, and both need to make short-term and long-term goals in order to have a successful relationship. In the end, it will be worth it.

James Wielder is a twenty-three-year-old graduate from Montego Bay Community College, where he studied Engineering Technology and lived in Rhyne Park Village with his father. We have been neighbors for over two years. I was a Customer Service Supervisor for a well-known Organization in the City of Montego Bay, a beautiful Parish filled with an abundance of nice sandy beaches, hotels, people, and countless attractions to choose from.

James waved every Monday, Wednesday, and Friday when I walked out to get in my car for work, but he never seemed unhappy - always smiling. One day, as I walked out, I saw him walking in the paved driveway, no shirt and his body slightly oiled and he had a bucket in his right hand and his car keys in the other. Admiring from a far I could see his small navel, his dark brown glossy eyes staring about and his hair neatly groomed. His pace towards the car reflects in slow motion as he observes different areas of his 2011 Burgundy Honda CR-V. I was caught in a trance. I didn't realize he was saying "Hello".

My question was how I would function knowing he has such an attractive body and he lives right next door. Next door to a dark chocolate, beautiful, seductive and horny single thirty-one-year-old African American who fantasizes daily about his bedroom techniques, using my sexual analysis to act as an indicator percentage for his character.

Releasing those thoughts, I quickly responded to him, gesticulating "Hey James" I anxiously answered. He looked and gazed for a moment and smiled. "I'm trying to clean this baby myself. Would you care to join me?" I laughed and said, " I would definitely help for sure if I wasn't working today, but I guess another day will do, right? Pouring water on the vehicle, he responded, " That would be some type of fun, huh?"

I proceeded to my car and drove off toot my horn and drove away. "How can I get that image out from my brain?" I thought. He's too young for me, I need a man, a strong responsible man, not that he isn't but, can he handle a woman as demanding as me? I thought about that all the way to work. My coworker Danny McFarlane greeted me in the lobby, and he stood in front of me and waved, "Hey, bad dream?" I smiled and respond, "tell me about it". He turned around and walked me to my office talking about how he wanted to invite me out for lunch and I kept on denying him or making statements like "I'm busy" but all this time all I kept seeing is James in my office unbuttoning his shirt waiting for the right moment and once he saw me he walked towards the door, pulled me inside, gripping my waist with both hands and I couldn't help but released my bag to the floor weakened by his touch, I put both hands around his neck and passionately kissed him. He then pushed me against the wall and pinned my hands above my head, kissing on my lips and neck as he released my hands slowly, I clutched them on his

15

face keeping those soft lips in place as he gripped my waist tighter and, squeezed on my buttocks.

TEMPTATIONS AND TRYSTS

"Liana!!! halloo, I saw hands waved across my face. Danny stood there looking at me "What's going on are you okay? You zoned out just now. Why not request some time off to relax or something? I think you're working too hard honey." I'm sorry, Danny I just have a lot on my mind. Please forgive me". He looked at me as I slowly walked around my desk and sat as he followed and leaned across and rested his right hand under my chin, lifting my face so he could kiss my forehead.

I'm leaving for lunch at twelve noon, and I'd love if you could join me, he asked. "I would love to, Danny, please just text or call me when you're ready, okay?" No, he replied, I'll be waiting for you right outside that door at twelve okay?" I smiled and nodded indicating my response. He touched my hand and then left.

Danny and I have known each other for years, but he's very sensitive, educated and very successful. He studied at Northern Caribbean University, majoring in Psychology. He lived most of his years in Kingston, Jamaica, since his mother wanted him to live with her after his Grade Six Achievement Test (GSAT). Being successful in his examinations, he was selected as the valedictorian for graduation at Success Primary and Junior High School in the Parish of Hanover after scoring 95% overall average earning a placement in Kingston College, where he continued his studies for five years. He met Andrea Cook in College where they started dating and got married within two years after which their daughter Brianna was born who is now eight years of age. Danny recently got divorced and is ready to commit again. He's always well dressed and has a smile to die for that just take your breath away, his eyes are dark brown with very thick eyebrows, shark shape nose and thin peach shade lips. He's a 5ft 6inches African American that wears a medium shirt and 34x30 pants and a size nine shoes. How did I know so much about this man? I wish I had the answer but unfortunately, I don't. My preference in man varies but I'm looking for a single guy, no kids and has never being married. Is that so hard to find I keep asking myself? I allowed my mind to process all unanswered questions as I focus a little on my workload trying to create an action plan for my team to submit by end of day to my Manager.

"Hey Liana," I immediately looked up and it was my coworker Beverly Small "Hey girl what's up?" I asked. She was smiling as she entered and closed the door "Girl you won't believe what happened to me last night, c'mon make a guess," she was smiling with excitement, "I can't even guess that right now, so please tell me what it is" I replied sarcastically leaning backward in my chair with my arms fold across my chest waiting for her exciting story. "Do you remember Thomas Sinclair I've been dating for a while now on and off, the guy you said was too self-centered for me? "Oh yes I remember him I respond quickly, you guys made up? "Beverly looked at me and said it's more than that, baby girl, so last night we went out for dinner; he took me to Seagrape Terrace at Half Moon Resort, where he had made a reservation for us at 8pm. The ambiance and food were amazing; it was a romantic evening world-class customer service given. After dinner we walked around the property and on the beach for a while kissing and catching up on old times. He told me how much he misses me and is looking for stability in his life and I would be the perfect woman if I accepted his proposal.

"Wait, wait, wait" I said to Beverly "did he propose, where's the ring?" I was too excited for her as she said "No Liana he didn't, he just wanted us to start over, I'm telling the story here just listen please" "Okay, okay I'm sorry go ahead" I said to her politely. I sat there gazing at her with my eyebrows raised and my lips clinched waiting for that moment when she gets to the juicy part about sex.

"Liana, she said, I wanted him as much as he wanted me so of `course I said "yes, we could start over and learn to appreciate our flaws or constantly communicate, trust each other, and have fun., right?!

We left the Hotel at about 11pm and he invited me to his home in Ironshore and asked that I spend the night. It took us approximately fifteen minutes to pull up in his driveway "We're here baby" he said and looked at me as I made an attempt to open the door he's such a gentleman he said "No, no, no Bev I'll get it" and stepped out quickly and avail himself to escort me out safely from the car, held my hand and we walked towards his building as he opened the door he glanced at me and said "welcome to our home from this day forward" I leaned forward in my chair as Beverly caught my interest and undivided attention with my hands forming a fist under my chin eager to hear what happens next. She kept on pacing back and forth in my office saying "Oh my God, oh damn" covering her face with both hands and started blushing, so I got a little annoyed and snapped her back to reality. "Beverly" I yelled can you please finish the story? Danny will be here any minute to take me for lunch" Okay, okay, she said. Before I knew it Thomas's lips were glued to mine and his hands massaging my breast gently, his right hand

22

immediately made its way to my love nest where I used my left hand to stop his soft hands from entering and asked that I use his bathroom. He agreed and offered a quick tour of his apartment flat before I went, while he set the moment with his favorite R&B souls' playlist of Brian McKnight hit songs.

His carpet, which covered his apartment floor, was coral and very soft. He had a glass table in the center with a lemon-green sofa and matching cushions. All the curtains were white with a touch of green in between. His kitchen was clean and well organized with bar stools and a winery. The paintings on the walls were art of nature and romance. The bedroom had a pole centered about twenty inches from the bed which has a leathery finish complimenting the drapes and walls. As I stared at the bed he walked up behind and kissed my neck, I turned around and asked, "how long has this been here?" "Just a few months ago" he replied. "Why would you have a pole here?" I asked, "I like to be entertained Bev, and you've always mentioned freaky sexual intentions that includes a pole, so I figured since we are changing for the better why not fulfill one of your desires?" As I stood there listening to him, I thought about removing my garments and put on a show working my way on that pole, but I second guessed it and figured I'll save that for later. "I'll be right back" I teased and went to the bathroom. "Don't be long" he yelled as I closed the door capturing an erection waiting for me as he walked away. I quickly freshen up, ready to expect the unexpected. As far as I am aware, he's excellent with his mouth all over.

I went back to the living area where he had candles lit and was standing with two glasses of wine in his hands, indicating that I take one which I did and went into his arms where we made a toast I took one drink and he drank his and ensured he shared his with me from his mouth. My body shivers as he kissed my lips, neck and breast, gripping my well curved glutes with his hands. I started unbuttoning his shirt and removed his belt while he ripped my dress apart, spreading my legs and pulled my red laced underwear aside to insert his index finger. I moaned biting his shoulder and kissing his neck at every stroke alternately kissing him passionately. Thomas suddenly lift me from the floor and placed me on the counter and tortured my love nest with his fingers and held my waist in position while enjoying the company of my breast in his mouth. I was dripping wet as he asked, "Tell me what you want?" I was super nervous as I wanted him to just spread my legs and place his soft lips between my vulvas, devouring my love nest while gripping my hips holding my body in position until I climaxed but instead I told him to make love to me. He said, "No tell me what you want me to do to you?" In a seductive voice while inserting his tongue in my ear, goosebumps covered my entire body as I begged him to taste her.

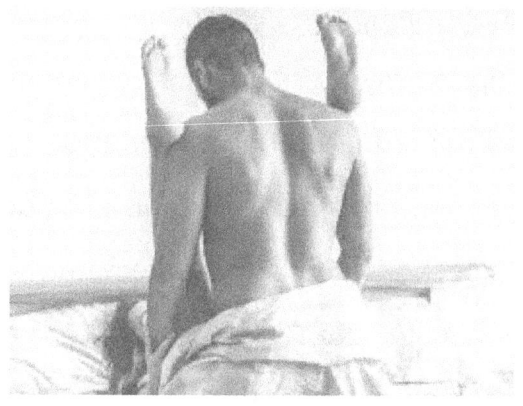

As my body temperature rises sweat poured down my face and chest wondering to myself how Thomas has improved tremendously since the last times, we made love, how did he know this is the type of love I needed? He licked my neck as I anticipated his warm mouth on my love nest and whispered, "like this?" "Yes, please yes" I begged. Thomas lifted my right leg on his left shoulder while kissing from my navel to my clitoris sharing his tongue with my hips as he slowly makes motions around my vulvas and inserts is tongue as I gasped at each stroke hovering his mouth completely drenching her dry. The pleasure was overwhelmingly suffocating as I calmly ask him not to stop until I made it rain, "come on baby" he said breathing heavily keeping the pace of his tongue and lips on my love nest. I closed my eyes tightly and screamed, holding his hands and arching my back. My legs were squeezing against his head as he holds and pulls them apart, keeping the intensity of the climax regulated to the end. I never felt so lifeless, so drained, as he gently helped me off the table and carried me to the bedroom and placed me on my back. A break is what I don't need, I said to myself and as hoped he came over me kissing my lips slowly as he gently penetrates my warm oven feeling every contraction of my fully developed walls with his rock-hard manhood. I moaned in pleasure as he slowly increased each stroke entering me deeper and deeper with his right hand under my neck calling my name "Damn

Bev you feel so good". He pulled himself away and twist me backwards spreading my legs ensuring I'm on my knees and face flat on the bed with my arms outstretched ready to receive him. We were sweating in pleasure, changing positions until I find myself on top. I could see his facial expression as he moaned in ecstasy increasing his blood flow throughout his body as his genital geared to ejaculate. I was not ready to stop so I quickly removed myself from his manhood and slide between his legs slowly hovering my mouth on his fully erected shaft swallowing him deeply as he yelled and shouted "Oh fuck, oh fuck Bev" I could feel the anticipation of his body eager to subside so I climbed back on top and rode him like never before as he attempted to spank my buttocks clenching my breast like a young cub until we both climaxed. "That was amazing" Thomas said, kissing my forehead as I rested my body on his and hugged him into a deep, romantic sleep.

Next day he took me home, and we confirmed moving in together next week.

"Wow" I said to Beverly "I'm so happy for you, that was an amazing night, wish I had a minute of that" we both giggled as I imagined James between my thighs. Immediately Danny knocked "are you ready?" "Yes I am" grabbing my handbag I looked at Beverly and smiled "I want to know everything from now on okay, love that story we'll talk later" she waved and said "have fun guys see you later" as I followed Danny to the car and left for lunch.

Danny was always punctual and argued how hungry he was, so we ventured to a popular restaurant called The Pelican on Gloucester Ave which is mostly called Bottom Road in the City of Montego Bay. I ordered oxtail with rice and peas and blended fruit punch and Danny ordered steam fish with white rice and fried plantains with fruit punch as well. As we sat there waiting on the food, he talked about us spending the weekend watching a movie or do a road trip visiting an art exhibition or something. I told him I would confirm the day but since we are coworkers it's unethical to have a relationship at work, but he insists and advised we will be very professional since we are both very responsible adults. I agreed and after receiving the meal he said "Liana I really care about you; if you just give me a chance to prove myself, I'll never disappoint you." I understand from a man's point of view when they hoped the next relationship would be different, but I looked at him and said, "Danny, I'm sure you thought the same when you got married years ago, and I really don't want to be another ex-wife." He was hoping I wouldn't make a statement like that about his life as I watched him sigh and looked away, but I was afraid of getting hurt again, so I mentioned it just so he knew I have limits and my intentions are to be considered seriously. He looked at me and said, "I can't change the past, Liana, only the future. It's the choices that make us who we are, and we can always choose to do the right thing." We both devoured our meal and commended the waitress on how delicious it was as she brought us the check with some mint candies.

On our way back, we talked about our career paths and how we can progressively make plans for the future, which will contribute positively to both our lives. He explained he would be resigning from the company in a few months to focus more on his business, and he would be better able to spend more time with his daughter and me since I proclaimed conflict of interest in the workplace would be an issue. I was surprised to hear this new story but was happy and sad at the same time, as I won't have another distraction at work. Things could, in turn, be in my best interest. I tried not to entertain the thought since he's on the borderline for my dream guy. Later that night I lay in my favorite T-shirt and a black lace underwear. I had made myself a ham and cheese sandwich and a hot cup of ginger tea sitting in my living room watching my favorite episode of the haves and the have nots by Tyler Perry when I heard a knock on the door. "Liana, are you home, it's James, can I talk to you for a minute?" "James!" I asked surprised "give me a minute, please". I hurriedly went to the bedroom and grabbed a night robe and unlocked the door, "come in "I said to James, how can I help? What's wrong? He was wearing a blue T-Shirt and blue jeans pants with a pair of sandals. "Can you take me to my office please I left my house key at work, I didn't drive today and asked a friend to drop me home after, my evening class at Northern Caribbean University but I can't get his phone and I need to get in my house?" he said nervously. "Sure, James I'll take you, where do you work?" I asked. "I thought you knew that all along Liana, I work at Half-moon Resort as an Accountant." I'm sorry

James I had no idea I smiled and said, "but I know where it is so let's go."

EXPLORING BOUNDARIES

On our way to his workplace, I asked, "How come you don't have a girlfriend? He looked at me with a smile and said, "That's funny you ask that, I ask myself the same question about you". We kept smiling at each other while I glanced momentarily on the road saying "I haven't found the right guy yet or maybe he hasn't found me. James stared with astonishment, smiling and shaking his head. He put his hand on his nose and, leaning his head backward, looked at me, but this time his smile disappeared. "What, why would you say that? James asked. I admire you every day from my window, and I haven't had the courage to tell you how beautiful you are. You're a great person, very ambitious, and any man would be lucky to have you as their partner. I was flattered by his statement and thought to myself I'm I too judgmental, do I need to just let things happen without thinking? James looked at me and I smiled and then he said "pull up at the security post let me talk to him ". As I entered the property and tried to locate a parking spot while James went to get his keys I turned off the ignition and quickly removed my underwear - I wondered to myself if this was what I really wanted, but to be honest, I was weak for him and wanted him so much. As soon as he came back, he suggested that we hang out for a while at a great spot in Greenwood Ironshore that he knew very well, but since I was still in my sleepwear I disagreed with hanging out anywhere public. My subconscious thoughts craved from within as the acceptance of passion flowed through my brain. We drove to a nearby beach at the border of Trelawney and Montego Bay, where we sat and talked for a while, but as we got bored, he wanted to do something exotic and crazy, so he asked that I drive back home. As I drove, he aggressively asked that I keep my eyes fixed on the road while he played with my love nest.

He inserted his tongue in my ear and his finger inside my love nest, stroking her indefinitely; the feeling was intense. I swerved to the left as he yelled, "Liana, please focus and keep your eyes on the road." I held on to the steering wheel with force and did what I was instructed to do, opening my legs wider as he rubbed his thumb against my soaked clitoris while stroking my love nest to a full, satisfying, intense climax. As the feeling of satisfaction subsided, I continued the journey home, parked, and looked at him, asking him to leave, but he insisted on inviting himself to my apartment, and even though I wanted to say "No," my body was calling him. Without further hesitations, we went inside, and James continued with his fingers, feeling the warmth and moisture of my love nest. He took his belt off and tied my hands behind me, and ask that I spread my legs open; he went on his knees and shadowed his lips on both vulvas, using his tongue to make strokes of passion and pleasure, breathing deeply underneath as my body anticipates multiple orgasms. He then moved me to the coach and transformed my position to the letter 'v,' where I sustained the prints of his palms against my gluteus Maximus, receiving the enjoyment of James kissing me from behind as I screamed and inflicted pain on my arm biting myself in pleasure creating a dynamic flow of secretion. I insisted on feeling his manhood deep inside as he deepened his tongue while alternately inserting his seven-inch erected organ inside with great force. Holding the back of my neck as he twisted and turned, increasing the pace of each stroke, making sure a constant secretion of orgasm was reached. I was overwhelmed with consensual sexual feelings. After a wild and enjoyable sexual intercourse, we hugged and just cuddled together to decrease the adrenaline rush that we created. In these moments our thoughts will then see the need to ask questions and learn more about each other. So I took the liberty of questioning his sexuality, so I asked him about his experience as a child. James mentioned he was very shy growing up, and going to school, he was sometimes teased, so his friends gave him a female that was seven years older to have sex with at the age of twelve, where he lost his virginity. They had sex every weekend and sometimes on Fridays when his mom worked late shift. Over a period of two years until, he left Kingston. In high school, he had multiple sexual encounters with teachers as he was very charming and smart. He spoke of a story where his Spanish teacher, Miss Simpson, offered to give him extra lessons after work but insisted that this be done at her cottage. When he went there, she was dressed in a short silky dress with no underwear on and sat around the table so he could see beneath using a marker drop teaser so he could see each time she bent over to pick it up.

James laughed as he claimed he lost focus and was brave enough to ask his teacher for a kiss, which she seemed upset about at first, but he calmly hugged her from behind and kissed her neck as she turned around to meet his soft paired lips while he placed her on the table to enjoy her heated embodiment with his veined erected manhood. She gripped his shoulder and squeezed him closer as he searched her love nest for her G spot, indulging completing to maximize multiple orgasms. That night, he learned nothing but was now his Spanish teachers' favorite student. They enjoyed each other's company throughout high school and accomplished his goal as a top student for the subject - how coincidental, if you should ask me - I thought. She ensured he had learned her subject while he took care of her sexual urges. He wasn't proud of what he did, but his teacher played a great role in his life, guiding his path to being a better love and a better kisser and inspiring him to always try to learn all he can about a woman before committing so as to gain experience in learning to appreciate their flaws and treasure their worth. The respect given to a woman is received by a man twice as much; he learned that the hard way. I was touched by his story and encouraged him to always try to do what's right. In return, he will never be disappointed as his decisions come from the heart. As much as I needed more of him, I would seem insensitive to proceed, but nevertheless, James began to get dressed, which saved me from what would have been an embarrassment.

"I'm sorry I can't stay. I enjoyed your company a lot," he said. In a sorrowful voice, I responded, "It's okay. I understand we'll have plenty of time, I imagine." Then I walked him to the door and kissed him good night. One of my favorite wines is the red wine Beringer Cabernet Sauvignon, so I went to my wine cellar and poured myself a glass, then went to bed at about ten-fifteen pm. It was 2am when my phone rang. The caller was an old friend of mine, Dalia Davis, but we called her "Peaches." She was furious, asking for my help and my accommodations for a few days. I could hear the frustration and fear in her voice, and of course, I accepted her request. It took her approximately forty-five minutes to get to my apartment, so I got up and prepared a place for her to rest and clean towels in the bathroom. I realize that as women, our true personality is hidden until we have a personal connection with someone who takes our breath away or that brings out our best interest. We think about a man so much when he is the best we've had in bed or have made a significant contribution to our life, contemplating how to show him how much we care. I was sad and happy as my thoughts about James were ruined by a sudden phone call changing the intentions of my desires.

Engulfed in my emotions, I lay on the sofa waiting for Peaches. Soon after, I was interrupted by a knock on the door. "Liana, it's Peaches." She said hurriedly I went to open it. She had a suitcase in her hand as she reached forward and hugged me. I took her to the living area and offered her something to eat or drink, which she refused as she sat on the sofa nonchalantly with tears running down her cheek. I sat with her and asked, "Peaches, please talk to me what's wrong?" She hugged me once more as roars of her cry echoed throughout the apartment. She was now safe, and without a doubt, the only option for her was to navigate her emotions in my arms. Assurance of comfort was to provide security for her uncontrollable feelings, in which the choice of words used is of utmost importance. I didn't know what to do; for the first time, I felt that I had failed to comfort a friend. She called out to me as she tried to explain what had happened. "I'm sorry that I showed up like this, Liana, but you're the only person I could call." as I looked into her watery eyes and dried the tears from her face, I said, "It's okay, Peaches, you know I'm always here for you, whenever you're ready to talk it's okay, mmmmhhh" she smiled and asked for a bottle of water. She began sorting through her items and changed her clothes to something more comfortable. She had bruises on her chest, face, and back. "Peaches, when do you want to see a doctor?" Ignoring my question, she said, "I'll be right back, ok. I'm going to use the bathroom." moments of silence went by, and nothing was heard, but the sound of her sobbing in the bathroom so I went and sat at the door, in tears asking that she talk to me. She was groaning from the bruises as she changed her clothes, and in a sorrowful voice, she said, "Bobby and I had a fight okay?" and suddenly opened the door and asked, "Can I get some wine, please?"

"Yes, of course, let's go to the kitchen so we can talk," I advised. I poured us both a glass as she said I love him so much I'll do anything for him just so he's happy, but it's never enough". Five years ago, we decided to live together. He's always optimistic about the future and our relationship, wanting to make each moment highlighted, fantasizing about expanding our sexuality limitlessly. Of course, I agreed to those terms and had gone out to experience some of these with him, but the problem was our relationship wasn't monogamous anymore. It's always a new level of illusion."

He always seems to make suggestions instead of asking, but I always ensure that he's pleased.

44

One Friday night, we went to a club called Taboo in the Parish and spotted Crystal Williams, a girl he claimed was his friend in college, walking over to us, excited to have crossed paths with us again. As she hugged me and waved "hello" to Bobby. We chatted for a while about old times until Bobby asked to speak with me privately while Crystal waited. He asked that we do a threesome that night with her; it would really make him happy. As hesitation transformed, my facial expression indicated that I would. On our way home, Crystal talked about her lifestyle after college and how she had become desperate to find true love but always seemed to find comfort in her former lovers. Right there and then, I wanted to tell Bobby to cancel, but I didn't want to spoil his night, so I figured it would be over soon, so why not. The evening was rather cool and relaxing as we had rain a few days before, and it was the winter season in early December. We got settled, and she asked to use the bathroom but looked at me and said, "Do you care to join?" Looking at her puzzled, Bobby added, "It's fine, Peaches, go; you need to relax." I went with her, and she closed the door behind us, "Are you nervous?" Crystal asked. "I'm not nervous," I responded, "I'm just curious as to why you seem so willing and agreed to have such an intense sexuality with us, and we've never talked about these fantasies before." She was rather bold and spoke confidently as if they almost planned the entire process. Always follow your intuitions; they are never wrong - I ignored the thought as Crystal explained she's been waiting a long time to fulfill her fantasy with someone as exotic, sexy, and fun as me. She walked close enough as I inhaled the mint from her breath, licking my lips as she passionately kissed them. She began removing my clothes and hers and led me to the shower. She placed my back against the wall as we enjoyed the moment of pleasure kissing and taking turns with our breasts. She caresses my love nest with her fingers and proactively kneels before me, lifting one leg to the corner of the bathtub and reaching beneath me with her warm lips flexing her tongue deep inside. I couldn't help but grab her head to keep it in position and put my body towards her as she grabbed my firm, wet glutes and secured my clitoris with her fully moistened tongue to slowly rotate beneath, stretching and kissing every part of my love nest. Suddenly, the enchantment of her touch devoured my body as sounds of sexuality fell from my lips, allowing Bobby to have us mesmerized by one of my favorite songs by Sevyn Streeter and Chris Brown, "It won't stop." The pace of the music captivated my thoughts as I moved in slow motion on her beautiful visage gasping at each turn moaning constantly until I climaxed. She kissed me and kept rubbing her hands between my legs "you taste great," she moaned. We then showered each other and, left the bathroom, and went to the bedroom to admire Bobby's muscular anatomy while he waited with a bottle of Ace of Spades champagne ready for us to enjoy toasting to a predictable evening. He grabbed and pulled me close to him, and we exchanged a romantic kiss like it was our first time together while Crystal occupied her oral cavity with his manhood taking it full length as she used her hand at times to alternate between each stroke. Joining her was evenly exclusive as we both wrapped our lips around his manhood, engulfing it as Bobby moaned at every touch.

I got up and walked to the bedroom and spread my legs, playing with my love nest and watching Crystal and Bobby enjoying the taste of their own juices. He asked that I position myself at the edge of the bed and kneel with my hands holding the cheeks of each glut, gasping upon receiving his fully veined eight-inch shaft as he gripped my waist and entered, slowly spanking as he deepened his manhood inside. Crystal climbed on the bed and ensured her love nest reached my mouth as I extended my tongue, rotating on her vulvas as she held on to my head, moaning with enjoyment. I turned on my back as Bobby took her warm mouth and placed her on his shaft, stroking her inconsiderably as I marveled in her love nest, stimulating a climax and making it rained on my face. It was my first time experiencing such unique sexuality - I loved it. We all laughed as I felt as though I was drowning. For about thirty minutes, we enjoyed each other, exchanging saliva juices and orgasms. Crystal spent the night and went home the next day while I went to work.

"Liana, Liana," Peaches said, "Are you falling asleep on me?" "No, no, I'm not. I'm just astonished," Liana said. It's puzzling that you came here crying, but nothing in your story dictates that breakdown. Did something happen afterward?" She turned away from me and sadly explained how she wished Bobby would marry her for all she has been doing with him; she is madly in love and wants no one else but him. However, it seems as though their relationship has expanded to a trio, as without another being sex between them is no fun. She was devastated, so I tried to comfort her and encouraged her to be optimistic and communicate with Bobby to conclude what level of relationship he preferred so she could plan going forward I said, Peaches, look at me, you should never sell yourself short for a man or anyone for that matter. Love yourself and make decisions that will be beneficial to your wellbeing and will give you peace who loves you first and makes decisions that are beneficial to your well-being. If it's his intention to change, he will, but never try to do that for him. You will need to set boundaries for your relationship, find activities that will entertain him so that his desires for another woman are demolished." "What would I do without Bobby,

Liana?" She paused It's been years of sacrifice, and all of this would be for nothing. I can't think of that right now. I have dedicated my time and patience to him; walking away would be the most difficult thing I'd experience."

"Do you know why I'm single, Peaches?" She looked at me and folded her arms. "No, I don't, Liana; why don't you tell me?" "Okay, I said, I'm single because I kept on thinking that including a man in my life would distract me from my own self. He would have my attention, my love, my loyalty for as long as he wants, showing him every day how much I care. No one knows me better than me, and if I meet someone with characters that dominate my interest, my initial thoughts will be to make him happy and believe me, that's what I will do. That night, we mirrored our experiences, and in the end, Peaches finally confessed what allowed her to show up at my doorstep in the middle of the night. Bobby has gotten someone pregnant and refuses to tell her who it is, and their heated

argument turns into a physical fight.

LOVE AND LUST

"Good morning, Peaches," I said, "did you sleep well?" she rolled over and glanced at me, covering her face with the pillow. "I think I did," she responded, looking horribly restless as she turned and lay on her stomach. I walked over to her and sat on the bed as tears flowed from her swollen eyes down her cheek. "It will be okay Peaches I'm here for you" I said kissing her on the forehead as I advised her to make herself at home and will check on her during the daytime. As I approached my Toyota 2019 Axio I saw James exiting his vehicle, but on his passenger side a bronze complexion, size ten, five feet, five inches, dark hair 'Chica' came out. To be honest at that moment I felt jealous, I felt betrayed and hurt. But why do I feel this way, why do I care to find out who she is? I needed to know so I went inside my car and called him hoping that he would answer but he took one look at his phone and rejected it. Then glanced over to my car and escorted his lady inside. I drove to work angry, furious and heartbroken. Thinking about a life with someone that didn't even know it. I never asked James about his personal life, and that was on me, a mistake that I made having a one-night stand with a guy I had fantasies about for years. How pathetic I am to even allow my emotional thoughts to occupy my brain for so long without preparing for the worst.

When I got to work, there was a spout of rose in a glass of water on my desk with a note - best Supervisor ever! I smiled, thanked the team, and proceeded with my daily task, immediately changing my mood for the day. Only to find out that none of the agents put it there, but my friend Beverly. We've been friends since high school; she was two years ahead of me, but somehow, we became friends. We used to take the same bus to school, Rusea's High, in the same Parish, but we never spoke to each other. Most kids our age would wave and say 'hi' if needs be back then. One day, I had a science project to do, gathering species of ferns. We lived in the rural parts of Hanover, consisting of hills and valleys of beautiful scenery, so getting the samples I needed was no problem. Using the Library to assist with the species, I saw Beverly walk in to return a library book called "The

Tower Treasures" by Hardy Boys. She glanced around the room, and we waved at each other and afterward proceeded to select a new book. "Hi, Liana," she said, what are you doing here? I looked at her and began to explain the project and the completion date, and she offered to help. That afternoon, we took the same bus home, and she invited me over as she had done the same project in the past, so she had some experience relating to the expectations of the teacher and the volume of information needed. I was very excited and immediately accepted her offer, which gave us more time to cement our friendship. I asked her mom, June Samuels, who is a grade seven English teacher at our community school, to contact my mom, providing her with my whereabouts and accompanying me home. When she came and saw Bev's mom, she was stunned as she mentioned they were best of friends in high school but grew apart and lost each other's contact after graduation as they had some boyfriend challenges back then - nothing they would want to talk about. Mom didn't try to make matters worse for us; instead, they hugged each other and laughed about old times, telling stories of adventures and misdemeanors. June gave us cornmeal pudding and a glass of milk for supper; it was delicious. Beverly is really smart. She has a great personality and always treats others with respect. I was able to complete my project within a week and got the highest score in my class at the end of the year. I was successful with seven of my subjects after sitting in the Caribbean Examination Council (CXC). Beverly was already in her second year. In college, she pursued a career in business management. She was successful and soon after landed a job in my company as the Site Manager.

"Damn, time went by fast," I mumbled as she walked into my office. "Hi, Liana, what's good?" She said, elated. Beverly was always in a good mood. I smiled and was introduced to a beautiful rock on her finger. I pointed at it and asked, "what happened here, he proposed?" She looked at me and replied, "This morning, when I woke up, it was already on my finger, and he was in the kitchen making breakfast. I called out to him, and he came with an egg omelet, strawberries, grapes, and a pegged orange with coffee in bed; after staring at me, he said, "I love you, B, and I prefer to have you forever as my friend, the mother of my kids and my wife." Liana, I was already crying Bev whispered in tears. I got up from my chair and hugged her tightly. "I'm so happy for you, sweetheart; you'll make a wonderful wife and great mom," I replied. "Thank you, Liana, but you know I can't go through the ceremony without you being my maid of honor, right?" With popping eyes and my mouth wide open, I was surprised she chose me, and excitedly, I accepted her thoughtfulness, reaching out with a hug. "I'll be honored; of course, I'll be your maid of honor," I responded. As I was left alone, my mind took me to an unhappy place that I had tried to forget for years. I remember the first time I was proposed to. I was twenty years of age. His name was Ray Rivers. We met at a restaurant I was working at the time in the parish. He was tall and light-skinned, with cut hair and a great body frame. We started dating, and at times I would stay at his place on weekends or days off. I would cook for him, massage his feet, tried my best at pleasing him in bed. But as vulnerable as I was indications of infidelity arises soon and when confronted all he would do is deny any of the allegations. Every time my suspicions rise, I always thought I was the problem, so I decided to do more for entertainment for him. I would dress up in lingerie and dance for him, take him to some of his favorite places, and whatever he wanted, I would fulfill his quest. But the game changed as soon as I started saying "no", no to oral sex, no to disrespect and lies, no to paying bills and giving money for gas. His interest suddenly changed, and he would stay out late at nights and when I called his phone no answer. I would text him, and he would be online on WhatsApp and read my messages and not respond. I knew few of his friends but no contact number so one day he came home, and I was sitting on the bed crying, waiting for him. He told me he loved me and I was the perfect woman for him. He's sorry for all the pain and suffering he has caused me and promised to do his best to change. We had great sex that night - yes, I opened the oven for him! All I wanted was him, so I dismissed the unfaithfulness and allowed good memories to take control of my mind.

The next day he went to work and called at about 3 pm and told me he's coming to stay the night and would prefer for me not to prepare any meal. He came home at about 8 pm with a bar of Cadbury chocolate, vanilla ice cream, a six-piece

KFC spicy and Barbecue Chicken combo, and a small box. He poured wine for us both and lit scented candles. "What's the occasion, I asked?" He looked at me and said, "I just wanted to show you how much I appreciate you." He portioned the food, and we ate and toast to a long-lasting relationship. He kneeled in front of me and proposed with a gold, single-diamond ring. Never have I felt so excited, so I said "yes," and he placed the ring on my engagement finger as we kissed and ended the night with rounds of pleasured sex.

I questioned myself a few weeks later: "Did he propose to build my confidence in him and forget about his flaws and his many moments of disappointments? But as weeks passed by, I realized the old Ray was back. Instead of not answering my messages, he would just agree to anything I asked and if I called, he would say, "I'm on my way, babe". Same lies but different concepts. "Why do I feel this way about Ray?" Is this love or the insensitive notion of a male stigma? I cried for days, nights mostly when he came home, and I wanted to talk to him or have sex, and he would say he was tired and turn his back and sleep. Once there's food in the house, his clothes are washed, and he has money to do whatever he wants, I'm invisible. I began to have second thoughts about that sparkling metal on my finger if I wanted to live in an unhappy relationship forever. Should I wait? I think I should. He would change. I know there's good in him." I keep telling myself that to satisfy my own insecurities. One day, I decided to show up at his apartment with the help of a friend. But he had no idea what he was up against. I told Eric I needed his help to take me to Ray's apartment to surprise him. I packed whipped creams and champagne and begged him not to say anything. We drove his car, and he called him, stating he was coming by, so I walked up to the door and hid while Eric yelled, "Ray". Astonished, a female opened the door wearing one of Ray's shirts. My eyes bled with tears as I pushed her and entered. Ray grabbed me, asking, "what are you doing here?" he looked at Eric and said, "What the fuck, man, how could you do this?" Eric raised his hands above his head and responded, "Listen, bro I had no idea, she called asking me a favor to surprise you, so I went along with it. I didn't know bro I'm sorry". Ray held me tightly to prevent any altercation with his mistress. She was standing in the corner with her arms folded, staring at me. Watching me in rage, looking crazy. At that moment, I dried my tears, took my ring off, and ask him why? He had nothing to say but he still wanted me, and he could change; I should just give him time. I walked away and asked that he stop by the apartment and collect his belongings that night. I couldn't eat, sleep, or anything; all I thought about was Ray and why would he hurt me like this? It took hours of counseling and the support of friends to get over Ray and even now he still calls and wants to make amends. I still love him, but it's better to accept someone's flaws then create new ones and try to adapt. The rest of the week was almost the worst for me I became obsessed with watching the famous Tyler Perry series "The haves and the have nots" and other comical movies. Just to keep my mind off my many relationship failures. I thought about how happy I would be if things had gone differently. Would I be happy or sad? The truth always comes back to haunt us at some point. I began drifting back to my childhood, wondering if I made a mistake or if I followed the rules of my ancestors or given a listening ear as a child. We never seemed to understand the restrictions created by our parents but were never hesitant to find out what would happen if we proceeded and ignored the rules that sometimes allowed us to be better men and women for future companions. I remember growing up, having a boyfriend was never one of my priorities. I was seventeen when I had my first boyfriend, who took my virginity - the most painful feeling I've ever felt. It happened so fast for a minute - I think - and I wasn't a virgin again. Christopher Gordon and I frequently kissed back then, and he would ask me to touch my vagina, and I should touch his penis. We would do that at our favorite hide away spot after school at least three times a day. I would lift my skirt up, and he would pull the underwear aside and rub his fingers over my vulvas until I was soaking wet while he kissed my lips. My small hands would enter his pants, massaging his penis until it was hard. One day, I was alone at home, and I told my mom Chris would be visiting to do some homework. She agreed, advising that my other siblings would be home shortly. Soon after, Chris came, and we hurriedly did what we always do, but as our sexual urges increased, I told him I would like to experience sex. He was very patient and tried to advise me of how painful it would be as he wasn't a virgin. I was so anxious I yelled, "Just do it! I want to feel it right now!" he looked at me and said, "Just relax, B I'll do something special for you first, and please don't ever mention this to anyone" without a doubt I promised I wouldn't. Chris slowly placed his head between my legs and allowed his warm tongue and mouth to do the trick as I tried closing my leg and begging him to stop. It felt weird but great at the same time, but the sensation was too much, and I didn't want to get carried away and get caught. So, he played with my love nest for a short while and asked, "Are you sure you're ready?" Then he opened my legs wider as he made his way between preparing to insert. I closed my eyes tightly and awaited the pain as I could feel his penis rubbing on my vulvas and my clitoris. His waistline bent backward as he inserted quickly instantly. I grabbed his waist, bite aggressively on his shoulder and yelled "please stop, it's too painful" I rushed to the bathroom, trembling in fear after seeing a small amount of blood, panicking that my mom will find out. Chris knocked on the door "are you okay, your brothers are coming?" I quickly opened the door and went to straighten the bed the way it was and opened our books, pretending to be studying. My heart and body were in pain I couldn't concentrate on anything educational that evening. All Chris did was stare at me in sadness hoping that nothing bad will happen or I will keep our secret, but I constantly glance at him reassuring that I'll be okay, and our secret is safe. He played a few video games with my brothers and then left. A few weeks later he asked that I see him after school at our usual spot so I went, and he told me how sorry he was and would love for us to continue our intimacy without sexual intercourse but indulge in oral sex. I told him I've never done it before and was not ready to start. But Chris didn't object; he wanted to ensure I kept my mouth shut about us, so he agreed to please me. For two years, occasionally, we do enjoy sex however, mostly oral sex in which he mastered overtime. By the end of the year Chris migrated to the United Kingdom and was never heard of again.

COMFORT IN COMPANIONSHIP

Suddenly I heard someone at my door "Liana
are you home?" It was Peaches "why are you crying
she said?" "Nothing honey, I'm fine," I responded.
She looked at me and asked, "Liana, talk to me, tell
me what's happening?"

I held my head down and told her about Chris and how sometimes I miss him and hoped that someday I could see him again, even if he's already married and has a family. Peaches hugged me and explained that she has gone through many decades of memories when she's alone and hoped I would find something to occupy my mind, so I wouldn't be thinking about the past.

Peach is a great friend, and she always knows the answer to many situations, which has guided me thus far as I developed self-confidence and motivation to persevere and continue throughout many days. So, as I listened carefully to her, I smiled and said, "I surely hope that I'll find love someday, but in the meantime, tell me about you and Bobby." immediately, her expression changed to a sad face, and she kept picking on her fingers. "That's a story, baby girl," she said, but I love Bobby, and I won't give up on him or our relationship no matter what." Peaches turned and looked at me and asked, "what would you do if your partner impregnates someone else after you've been trying for years?" Looking at her, I could see how devastated she was, and I cautiously tried to give her my honest opinion. "Peaches, I sadly looked at her, holding onto her hands. I would try to make it work if he's a good man to me and, honestly, if I genuinely know that I'm at fault. But if he wants to go, I won't stop him." She shook her head and walked away and kept looking through the window. "I appreciate your honesty Liana," she said, but I searched Bobby's phone and found a positive pregnancy test result, and when I confronted him, he stated Crystal is pregnant. "Liana, I had to ask Bobby how it happened. Was he having a secret affair with her? He looked at me and walked away, and I chased him and kept hitting him from behind. He turned around and used the back of his hand to hit me across my left cheek and yelled, "Don't ask me anything. All I did was take care of you, and no matter what, a child seemed impossible, but until you can do that, it's over!" I lay there on the floor crying as I could hear the loud shouts of him leaving the room and driving away.

As I listened to Peaches, tears fell from my eyes. How do I comfort a woman who has heard those words from a man she's madly in love with, knowing she's at fault? As the words "Peaches, I'm sorry" fell from my lips, all I could do was hug her and promise better days to come. One of the hardest truths to swallow is infertility, especially when your partner aggressively expresses how he feels and is willing to move on without a discussion. Even the brave need encouragement and love, so I played my role as a friend. Sometimes, we hold on to a fight that's not our own. We are challenged by our own shadows, and it terrifies the fear within. Women love deeply most of the time, and we fall in love with different areas of a man forced to ignore his flaws. In desperate times, we'll fabricate a plan to activate our inner thoughts, carving a new formula of intended happiness that is non-tangible. Some of us can overcome situations like these easily, but not all can move on in an instant - love takes time to heal, as the famous song writer Celine Dion sang.

Peaches cried herself to sleep, and I stood up all night on the sofa with the television light flickering as I stared into wondrous worlds, seeking answers. My love life is a roller coaster, and hoping for change. Peaches' experience gave me a wakeup call. By morning light, she was up making breakfast as tunes of her melody filled the air. I got up and joined her as we sang, "Britt Nicole, sun is rising." Tears filled her eyes as she hugged me and cried. "Do you know what? I want to do something today instead of staying home?" I asked. She agreed to walk in the park on Gloucester and on the beach just to clear her head and maybe a movie afterward. We ate and left, but mentally, she was not sitting next to me. It was a beautiful day, filled with the warmth of the smiling sunlight and happy faces. She smiled as we came to an intersection and saw a police officer and a taxi driver arguing, causing massive traffic to pile up due to an accident. However, the driver of the car had some outstanding tickets and was begging the officer not to prosecute him as he shouted for help. As I pulled up and found a parking lot close by, we changed our clothes into beach wear, but Peaches then changed her mind that she would like to go to Doctor's Cove Beach, so we drove there instead. It wasn't far away, and even so, I would take her anyway. We rented umbrellas and chairs to relax on the beach and a few alcoholic smoothies to help with relaxation. Her face changed from sadness to deep emotional thinking. She took a few deep breaths and looked at me momentarily as I occasionally asked, "are you okay?" And she would respond with a smile, "I'm okay, hon, this too shall pass." She got up a few minutes, went to swim, and then came back saying she wanted to go home and rest. I rescheduled watching a movie for the following day and took her home.

As soon as I got up to leave my phone rang, so I picked up and answered.

"Hi Liana, how are you? Is Peaches with you?" Bobby said as I responded, "Oh I was wondering whose number this is. Peaches is with me, yes, but I doubt she wants to talk to you. Did you call her? He then responded to me, "We've been friends ... immediately, I interrupted him. "Hell no, Bobby, we're not friends; you happened to be fucking my best friend, and the moment you put your hands on her, you lost my respect." He was furious. "Liana, you listen to me now, remember this, okay, I know where you live; when I come over there, tell it to my face!" Bobby hung up on me after that statement. Peaches looked at me and said let's go please. I was sadden by her response and got up and followed her to the car.

I'm so sorry Peaches, I said, looking at her facial expression as she looked straight ahead towards the car.

It's ok Liana I know you're trying to help, thanks for standing up for me, she replied with a smile.

Even though we seemed to enjoy a beautiful evening, I could see that she was in a different world, trying to understand why this unfortunate situation landed on her door and ruined her relationship. When we got home, she immediately exited the car and rushed to the bathroom to get rid of all the sand in her hair and skin.

As I listened to the water running from the shower, I breathe deeply and thought about how this hurt would affect her and how I could be of help to her and enjoy our friendship once more. They say time heals all wounds, but for her, it may take additional resources to get her back to herself again. As I searched through my thoughts for answers, my phone rang with another strange number and my guess was, I bet this is Bobby. Since Peaches was in the bathroom, I thought, now is the time to answer him a different way so on the third ring I asked "what do you want? Bobby was silent for a second, Liana he said, I'm sorry about earlier but I really need to speak with Peaches and of course I declined his request and yelled "stop calling me" then ended the call but I didn't know she was listening to my conversation with Bobby the entire time. She was so nervous and scared a 911 call was made, and since the scar was still visible on her face, she could file a police report for domestic violence. The operator advised the police would be there in fifteen minutes. Within seconds, screams of tires were heard outside. It was Bobby in my driveway yelling for Peaches. "He must have lost his God damn mind," I yelled. "Peaches, Peaches," he called, "open the door, Liana, before I break it down!" As afraid and frightened as I was, I shouted, "The police are on their way, so leave now." "It's cool, I'll leave, Peaches I hope you keep hiding, and Liana I hope you know who you're defending," he said as he got in his car and left. The police came and I went out to talk to them, but Peaches was hesitant and asked that I don't mention anything to them just give them a story that some guys got the wrong address and came by the house but left. I didn't question anything bad she was in shock and I wanted to do what's best for her but to report domestic violence the abuser will need to be able to make a report and follow through and I can't do that for her. I hugged her and told the officers just as she said, and they took the statement and left.

"Hi Liana, its Bobby, please don't hang up, I need to speak with Peaches please." Without saying anything I hang up.

I walked to the bedroom and asked, "Peaches, did you talk to Bobby?" She shook her head and said, "I don't want to talk to him." I sat with her for a while and tried to convince her to do so; maybe it will help. Bobby may have an aggressive personality but something about the statement he made had me wondering about that night Peaches showed up at my place. I never questioned her; instead, I provided comfort. She continued to reject Bobby's calls and began preparing herself to resume work the next day. She continued her days as normal, as if nothing happened.

One afternoon I got home a little earlier than usual to have an electrician checked on my power supply as I've noticed a shortage whenever I plug my iron in and used the microwave at the same time. To my surprise when I drove in James was standing in his driveway talking on his phone he glanced at me and I heard him say "let me call you back" then called out to me "Liana, Liana, please I want to talk to you" as I closed the door of my car the heat of anger rushed through my veins. I took a deep breath and with a stern face I responded, "Hi James, how can I help you?" He became frozen, looking at me as he tried to find the right words to say, then "boom" it came out "Liana I know you saw me the other day, but I'm really sorry I didn't tell you before that about Jessica, my girlfriend." He clasped his hands and made a step closer to me "I didn't mean to misguide you into thinking we'll have a relationship. Jessica and I had a fight and you were at the right place at the right time and yes it was fun, I enjoyed every bit of you, but we can't be together as much as I want to" he explained. I looked up at him and said, "You never misguided me, James. I wasn't expecting anything different I was just surprised that's all." As my mind lingered with a question I asked, "did you ever had feelings for me?" "Yes, yes Liana I always do" he quickly responded, walking closer to me as if he wanted to touch my face but stopped and stepped backward, saying "I'm really sorry okay?" I nodded at him, acknowledging his apology as he walked away, to his apartment.

I went inside and the electrician was almost through. About thirty minutes later he had me try again to ensure his work is done properly. Which I did and everything seem fine, so I paid him for his work and then he left.

As tired as I was, I decided to have a bubble bath and relax with some wine and music. Laying there with one of my favorite glass of Rashi Claret semi sweet red wine, thinking about James hands over me desperate to fall in love. "Oh the things I would do to make him focus on only me," I thought to myself, this feeling of desperation needs some Trey songs but instead I played Marques Houston's "Sex with you", placed the glass on the floor, and spread my legs, while playing with my love nest and taking turns rubbing my nipples and thighs pouring water all over me - just enjoying the moment. As I combed my nipples with my tongue, feeling the warmth of my mouth, I inserted two fingers inside, moaning as I repeated the strokes. I held my head back and my eyes closed, gasping for breath as I got closer to a climax.

"Oh damn, what are you doing here?" As I looked up it was Peaches staring down at me. Feeling so embarrassed I tried to cover myself. "Liana it's okay" she said, I'd love to join you". "No, no Peaches please don't take your clothes off, please!" I begged. Before I knew it, she was naked and immediately stepped into the bathtub, putting the bottle of wine to her head. I've never been with a woman before, and the thought of doing so with my best friend was outrageous. She came over me and started kissing me and removed my hands from between my thighs. "Peaches stop please I can't do this." as she kissed my neck and inserted her finger - she touched my G spot and I gripped her shoulder, gasping and wished she'd never stop. "Do you like that, I bet you don't want me to stop now, right?" I didn't want her to, it felt so good all I wanted to do was climax and she was doing a damn good job setting the pace. She gripped my neck and increased her strokes, using my soft breast as popsicles. Her lips were soft and gently moving across my body, including my ear and neck. She was breathing intensely and told me she wanted to taste me so bad but was waiting for the right moment.

"Peaches, I can't do this?" I asked myself why not? Why not let her enjoy me and I enjoy her? But I was nervous I didn't want to seem so easy; I didn't want her to be convinced I'm at least interested. "Just relax, let me make love to you" she said. How can I resist that? I was anxious to feel this experience I've only thought and heard of by friends and some popular websites. So, I got up and followed her to the bedroom where she used a towel to dry all unnecessary fluid using her tongue to harden my nipples and clitoris. I moaned in pleasure holding her head in place as she makes circular motions on my vulvas, inserting her tongue and kissing her gently. "Oh, fuck Peaches, don't stop. I'm almost there, oh my God" I gripped the sheets and kept on lifting my hips to feel her lips and tongue deeper inside. My eyes were in tears as my body awakened to a remarkable climax. My knees were weak, and I was out of breath as Peaches gently massaged my love nest with her tongue. She did it, I never thought she could, but she did, and it felt so good. I've had oral sex before but nothing like this feeling. I didn't feel for sex after all I wanted to do was sleep, my body was drained - her lips were enough.

Catching my breath, we cuddled as she kissed me gently. I looked up at her and asked, "How long ago did you feel this way about me, or have you always liked both sexes?"

"I do, Liana, I just didn't want to ruin our friendship, but I've always wanted to know what it feels like to be with you" she said. I was speechless and told her I've never been with another woman, but I'd like to try. I questioned myself always when I'm uncomfortable but curious about a situation - and this was my curiosity answering wanting to taste and touch the body of my own.

I was super nervous as I began teasing her vulvas with my lips. Spreading her legs to initiate a stimulation using my warm mouth on her beautiful organ. Gripping her waistline to keep her body in position as I matched her motions desperately awaiting a climax. She was gripping my head as she made a fist with her hand begging me not to stop. As hesitant as I was, I try to condition my mind entirely to the moment of pleasure feasting on her love nest to reach my goal. She guided my hands and lips where she wanted to as I suspected she is an expert at love making. She was gasping for breath and her mouth opened wide with her eyes closed tight. As she gripped the sheets and screamed, "I'm coming, I'm coming, oh fuck!" Ounces of fluid covered my face as she made it to the finish line breathing intensely, trying the catch her breath. "Liana please I need a bottle of water" Peaches said. I hurriedly went to the kitchen and grabbed a bottle for her watching as she drank it all at once. Calmly breathing as she lay on her side, she immediately entered sleep mode.

I watched her sleep for a while, then left to take a shower, relaxing in the bathtub, thinking about my experience with Peaches. Vodka always sets the pace after good sex, so I decided to pour myself a glass on the rocks, tune my Television to Netflix and watched "Avengers - Endgame" until I fell asleep. I must have watched that movie a hundred times.

MORNING DILEMMAS

The sunlight from the kitchen window woke me since I have fallen asleep in the sofa, I rushed to get ready, knowing that I'll be late for work anyway. Within minutes I got dressed. Peaches was still sleeping so I left her a note and rushed through the door. When I arrived, Danny was in the parking lot smoking a cigarette that was almost finished. He then threw it to the ground and stepped on it to put it out, he yelled, "Liana, how are you doing, I haven't seen you in a long time?" I smiled and said,

"Hey stranger" as we embraced each other with a kiss on the cheek. The strong scent of the cigarette over shadowed the calm scent of his perfume, killing the overall taste of his aroma. We walked to the entrance and before we took the elevator, he suddenly kissed me within fifteen seconds I pulled away. I looked at him astonished and he said, "I've always wanted to do that, now you'll have something to think about". The door of the elevator slowly closed as I glazed upon his handsome face, lost for words. It's not surprising that he wanted to kiss me but surely not at work - that's where I would set boundaries, my boss could catch us, and I could lose my job. What was I thinking allowing him to do that? No wonder he was looking over his shoulders as we stood there waiting. I need to talk to him; I know I need to, or this could be a whole different channel of romance I didn't plan for.

Walking towards my office, Beverly and her Assistant, Clare Clarke, approached me. "Hi Liana, you okay, you look lost in your thoughts."

I'm doing okay, Clare" I responded.

"No lipstick this morning, or did someone kiss some off?" I looked at her and smiled as Beverly asked, "Did you see Danny? He was asking for you?"

"Yea, I just saw him in the parking lot" I responded. "Oh Liana" she looked at me with a raised eyebrow, "did you guys kiss? Why there's isn't much lipstick on your lips?" I rolled my eyes and stared at her "Oh my God Bev, are you really doing this now?"

"Yes we are Liana, so tell me what happened!" I took a deep breath and answered "Okay okay, we kissed for a short while okay, no big deal" Applying my lipstick back, "see I'm all good now, right, lipstick on".

90

"Can I ask you something Bev?" I added as she instructed her assistant, Clare to leave. "I really like Danny, but I'm not sure if I should date him, - I don't want to fall in love and get hurt again based on his past. What do you think?"

Bev knew how vulnerable I was, especially when I was in love with someone. But truth is my defensive hormones will be erupted once I allow anyone close. I'll keep my guard up for as long as it takes. "Liana, I understand, but a leap of faith doesn't hurt sometimes. Get to know him; he's an amazing guy," Bev said convincingly. "Yea, I guess you're right, I'll see about that" I responded in a soft voice. As she opened the door to leave, she quickly said "I'll talk to you later, honey, I have a meeting in a few" then she left.

Just out of curiosity I called Danny "Liana, I'm really sorry about earlier," he said at the first ring. So, I asked "What are you apologizing for?" I want to know why you are so interested in me?" He was silent on the phone for a while and then answered "you are smart, intelligent, kindhearted, respectful, independent and beautiful and trust me I have a long list but just to name a few. I won't hurt you Liana and for sure I want to make you happy. As long as it takes, I'll wait for you, I'm not asking for a decision right now." But just something for you to think about, okay."

Digesting all he said, I was amazed and went to ask, "Are you looking for a short term or long-term relationship?" Without hesitation he responded "A woman like you deserve the best; thus the reason I'm pursuing you, I would never think short term. I'm desperately in need of a long-term gig, and if that doesn't work, I want nothing more than your friendship. I'm ready, Liana, and I want you".

I was gripping my chest and biting my lips feeling like a teenager again as my mind reflect on the predominant emotions yet again consuming my thoughts, confusing my inabilities to make a decision. Nevertheless, conquering the elements of failure, I immediately surrendered and sought to find loves calling and the silence was broken as I added "Danny, I'm sure you'll give me the satisfaction I need as you're a gentleman, thank you for being so kind to me and I hope someday we will laugh and remember this" Me too Liana he said as we left our pondering minds floating.

It was a beautiful day, sun was out at its best and the streets filled with pedestrians and motorist, horns tooting everywhere. I looked out my window and was super excited or must I say astonished to see a long last friend. He was dressed in dark blue jeans, black shirt and a mustard jacket. His watch created rays from the sunlight as he combed his way through the crowd. It was Chris, my high school sweetheart. I couldn't believe it, "was it actually him" I asked myself. I stood and watched as he went to the coffee shop across the street. I quickly grabbed my jacket and ran to the elevator, as I wait to cross the street - damn the light took forever to change, my heart beat has now increased, I rushed to the coffee shop and hurriedly opened the door and looked around slowly but he was nowhere to be found. My eyes were filled with tears as moments of reflection deteriorated my mind. I became nervous and hollow inside. It's been years, and without a doubt Chris seem irreplaceable. All I could do was walk back to my office and imagine the look on his face or our faces when we see each other. "Wow, it has been fifteen years" I thought deeply as these were unscrambled by Clare "Hi Liana, how are you? I have these papers for you to complete by end of day" thanks Clare I responded. "Have a nice day and thanks for interrupting my thoughts I said jokingly. She giggled and then left.

As I drove home from work, I felt rather nervous since Peaches called and advise she was cooking and asked that I stopped at the supermarket and grab a bottle of red wine Serbanet Sauvignon on my way home. She greeted me at the door and pulled me excitedly to the kitchen to show me what she was cooking and how she did all that for me as a surprise. "Peaches you didn't have to do this, but I'm grateful - thank you." smiling at her as she responded, "I know Liana, but I love you, and I want us to be together". "Peaches, I responded shaking my head slowly as I looked at her beautiful eyes filled with tears. "Liana please," she said just try it and see; what if we were meant to be together? Why all this happened did you think about that?" She added. Peaches - I looked at her and said, "let's focus on dinner for, now shall we?" I'll give you my honest opinion in a short while okay" I wiped her tears and said, "now let me get those clothes off, I'll take a shower and be back to enjoy all this delicious meal you've prepared". She was elated and smiled "sure Liana" I'll get this wine chilled by the time you get back". I went to the bathroom and sat there thinking to myself that I'm in so much confusion with relationships of both sexes. I kept on leaving an impact on whoever I was around. It was not my intention for Peaches to be misled by my sexuality. How did I get to this point? How can I fix this? She had fallen in love with me. My best friend has gotten the sensation and passion from me; she yearns for so much in a man. I felt sorry for her thinking I should have said "no, just no". But I allowed my body to think for me, and now I'll have to fix this addiction of sexuality

96

between us. Every time I close my eyes, I remember our passionate time together and beg my mind to hit the delete button and make it all go away. I hopped in the shower and cleanse my body and tried to forget but it was the hardest thing yet, as this is where it all started in this damn shower I recalled placing my head against the wall sobbing as I burst into tears. "What I'm I going to do?" I asked myself.

"Liana, are you okay, you've been there for a while?" Peaches asked. I quickly dried my tears and wash my face and answered, "I'm okay Peaches, I'll be there shortly". Before I could finish my sentence, she came rushing through the door. "I'm fine" I said as she handed me a towel. "Are you sure" your eyes are red, and you're congested," she added. Drying my face, I explained "I got too much soap on my face and I got some in my eyes" I took a deep breath and said, "Peaches I'm fine I promise". She held on to my hand and said "let's go eat before the food gets cold" I need to get dressed, I responded. "No, it's fine you don't need to Liana it's just us here, come on let's go. I shook my head and went with her and she pulled out a chair for me and guided me to sit around the table. She brought the food and wine and said "let's bless this food" she prayed and then we dived in. She cooked shrimp pasta, basic tossed salad, and boiled chicken breast. The wine was super cold and made everything super tasty. It was Cabernet Sauvignon which had a medium sweet flavor that sent shock waves through my body. "This is very delicious Peaches" I smiled. "Thanks, Liana."

Peaches had two glasses of wine already, and when she made that statement she was staring in suspense. She then went under the table and grabbed my legs open. Previous restrictions surfaced to reject her needs, but my body wanted her, and Peaches knew at that moment I'm vulnerable and that was her queue to take advantage. I took a deep breath as I gasp at her kisses and gentle romantic touch, keeping her momentum at minimal knowing the intensity of the climax and the effect of each tease mixed with saliva juices streaming with orgasms. My body struggled to maintain its position on the chair as I leaned backward, as my breathing increased, tolerating the dynamics of an emotional sexual torture. Excitingly she ripped the towel and inserted her middle finger as I balanced the chair to the kitchen counter and gripped her head holding the position of a perfect feeling where I managed to successfully reach another climax.

I whispered in a seductive tone "Oh fuck I did it again" I whispered to myself as Peaches came from under the table and helped me to the sofa to relax but she didn't stop there. She played with my nipples and kept kissing my lips, belly button and hips. I was extremely hopeless and wanted her to stop but I couldn't get the words out. She went down to my love nest and kissed her gently with her tongue and lips closely rubbing both all over her. My heart was pounding, and my body was seeking refuge from the intensity of the seduction - or should I say unraveled sentiment. Peaches were using the opportunity to open my thoughts to her feelings towards us and desperately seek for ways to ensure I believe that we could be together. I held her face and begged her to stop and surprisingly, she did as I closed my eyes and fell asleep right there.

When I woke up it was 9:30pm and I was covered with a blanket. My head was pounding, and I was starving, so I got up and went to the kitchen made myself a plate and devoured all with a bottle of water. As I stood in-front of the kitchen sink to complete washing the dishes, Peaches walked in with a sad look on her face and sat on the kitchen counter. Liana she said "I'm really sorry about earlier but to be completely honest I love you and every day it feels different; when you smile, it takes the pain away and you always know the right words to say when I'm at my lowest point. You never judge me, Liana and for that, I'm grateful to have you as a friend but it would be perfect if we were together." Peaches poured her heart out and at this point I was lost for words; I didn't know what to say and she was weeping bitterly with tears. All I did was hugged her with tears in my eyes and said "we'll get through this one okay, we will find love and I'll make sure that you have a partner before I settle with anyone okay" she nodded, and I added "I promise". She then pulled away and explained "One thing I can't promise you Liana is that I will stop loving you and until that day I will forever bring you to your knees when I make love to you. All I want you to do is just enjoy the unforgettable pleasures offered to you since we both have a date with true love. We both giggled and went to the bedroom, where we cuddled, watching "The Other Woman," directed by Nick Cassavetes released in April 25, 2014; we gave our views on a few areas then we both fell asleep.

THE UNRAVELING STORM

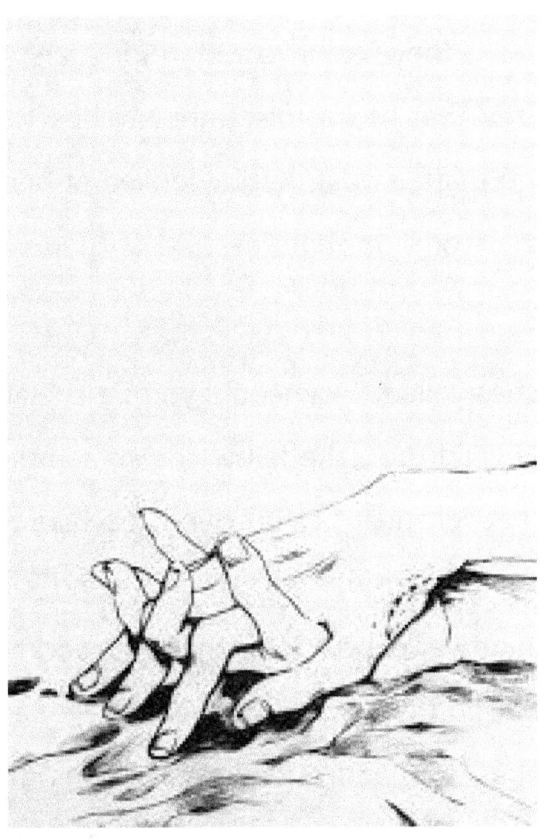

For the rest of the week Peaches behaved well, she tried hard not to allow her emotions to interfere with our friendship. She made a few advances but nothing too extravagant. She developed the courage to see Bobby at their apartment to talk to him about their relationship, she wanted him to end his affair with Crystal and resume what they had invested in for years as she emphasized that he promised they will be together forever no matter what. Bobby looked at her angrily and said "I won't do that Peaches. Crystal is carrying my child"

Peaches yelled "How could you be so selfish, I wanted a child too." she fell to the sofa and began crying. "I never meant to hurt you" he said, but you left me no choice since we've been trying for years and nothing happened. It's either you work with Crystal having my baby or you leave." He has given her an ultimatum and of course she would not accept that instead she was verbally abusive. Trust me; love will do that to you if you're loyal to the wrong person.

As I wait outside in my car, I heard loud shouts and screams from Bobby and Peaches. So, I got out and ran to the door and tried to open it, but it was locked. Peaches was shouting at Bobby to stop she yelled "stop it" I peeped through the window and saw his hand raised above his head and punched her. I continuously banged on the window and yelled for him not to hurt her and open the door. I had no choice but to call 911. The response time was quick as they arrived within fifteen minutes. During that time Bobby was swearing on top of his voice and Peaches lay on the floor of their bedroom crying. Officers came, and he opened the door with his hands on his head "don't shoot" he said as officers apprehended him and placed him in the back of the police vehicle. I rushed inside to attend to Peaches. She was bleeding from her nose and mouth same as the night she came to my apartment. As the paramedics quickly assisted her, I stood there looking around and to my surprise Crystal was standing in the hallway drowning with tears, holding her dress in a fist position across her chest as if she was having a heart attack. "I'm sorry," she said sobbingly.

I stared at her with deep disappointment, "what I'm I suppose to do, walk away? I questioned my thoughts as I covered my face with my hand. I can't be so selfish; I can't just ignore her as much as she partially destroyed a beautiful relationship. I slowly walked towards her and she came and hugged me tightly sobbing like a baby without her mother. "Liana I didn't set out to intentionally hurt anyone, I'm so sorry for all of this." I looked at her and said "it will be okay. Just find the time to talk to Peaches she's the one you should be apologizing to right now, I need to go to the hospital to be with her so take care of yourself okay"

I ran outside and followed the ambulance to the hospital. She was still conscious, and the doctors took her through ambulance triage, where they assigned her a bed after completing her vital

106

signs. The bruises were severe based on the doctor's prognosis, so she was admitted for three days until her eyes opened and the swelling decreased from her jaws. Later that night, the police officers from the Freeport police station came to take our statements and advise that he would be charged with assault occasioning grievous bodily harm. They didn't stay that long but seemed very sensitive towards the situation and confidently mentioned that they would be in touch if additional information was needed.

I stayed with Peaches all night every day providing her with the support she needs and tried to gather more information about her relationship with Bobby and Crystal. It's not connected. Why would Bobby get Crystal pregnant if he knew the relationship would cause conflict between them both? What is Peaches hiding from me? Or is she hiding anything? My suspicions went off like an alarm clock, and I was desperate to find answers.

Peaches was in no mood to talk, and she kept quiet the entire time we were there, but on the second night, she had a visitor, Robert, Bobby's best friend. He came by to check up on her and brought her some fruits and juice. He mentioned, "I know how things are with Bobby, so I am doing my part for him" he kissed her on her forehead and left. She thought she would be out on the second day, but the doctor recommended an additional day in which he wrote a leave of absence note for her to take to her employer. The following morning, I dropped off the letter at her workplace. The news was all over as I showed up, I could feel the eyes of gossipers piercing ahead as I walked towards the building. Some approached me and asked about her condition, but I assured them she was doing well. Others wanted to visit, but I knew what Peaches would say she is in no shape to entertain a group. I would know, I've been trying to do that for the past couple days. My suggestion to her coworkers was to have an edible arrangement done with a get well soon card sent to my address and I'll ensure it's received - "she would be grateful," I added.

After she was discharged, she decided to stay home for a few more days. She wanted to be left alone and recover emotionally so I honored her request and instead of staying home with her I left for work. When I went to work, I sat in my office and all I wanted to do was screamed. I wanted to cry but all I had was my computer screen reflecting a sad and broken imagine of what is left of a strong black woman. I placed my hands over my face trying to hold the tears back when suddenly Danny walked in. He knew from that moment I needed a friend, someone to hold me and a shoulder to cry on. He looked at me with stretched arms to welcome my overwhelming emotions of sadness as the tears rushed down my cheek. The feeling of being safe and protected - I don't know what to do

Danny. How can I help Peaches? She's been through so much, and yet every time I think she has overcome a challenge, another emerges.

Danny held me tighter and whispered "It will be alright, I'm here for you"

"Thank you Danny I really appreciate you being here for me"

He held my face and asked Liana, are you sure you can stay today? Would you like to take the day off?"

"No Danny it's okay, thank you but I can manage, besides Peaches wants to be alone for a few days I wouldn't want to break her concentration.

Exiting the office with Danny I went to the restroom to get myself together then proceeded to my daily routine. On my meal I saw Beverly she was dressed in a red dress with black jacket and black stilettos, showing off her modeling skills. I had to smile as she walked up to me.

"What do you think "Do I have a chance to enter the modeling industry?" she joked; my smile was wider than before as I giggled "Girl, you rock for sure".

I tried not to spoil her moment of joy or burden her with Peaches' tragedy. So instead, I took a deep breath and provided my undivided attention to her as we discussed plans for her future.

She sat with me and advised of plans for the wedding and wanted some help with choosing Color and decors. She had hired a wedding planner but needed my presence as I should be there since I'm the maid of honor and we could make final decisions together. We set a date for the following week, which was agreed upon to do some tasting.

Danny walked by and Beverly asked, "Are you coming to my wedding as Liana's plus one?"

Danny and I looked at each other and before I could respond he answered "of course I will be Bev" he kissed me on my forehead and said "I'll leave you ladies right to it" and walked away.

Bev was seemingly enjoying the moment as she claimed she has gotten her heart desire of things changing between Danny and me. As she walked away, she said "we should have a double wedding, see you later Mrs. D" as she modeled down the pathway.

Smiling at her as she walked away, I sat and thought of Danny, wondering if I should consider dating him. Having a rebound relationship is unfair- I don't think I'm ready. I quickly erased the thought and called Peaches, "Hello Liana "

Hey Peaches how are you?"

"Yes I'm fine except that when you get home I won't be here, okay I need some time alone."

Listening to her I knew something was off so I tried convincing her to stay.

"Peaches please stay; we'll get through this together"

"Liana I'll be fine I couldn't thank you enough for what you have done for me as a friend and is grateful for the moments we shared but I promise you, I'll be okay I need some time just to clear my head. I love you, Liana always and forever"

The line went dead. I thought it was a bad connection, so I yelled "Peaches, Peaches, are you there?" I looked at the phone screen, and the call had ended.

My heart was pounding, and I became nervous. I immediately rushed to the parking lot and drove to my apartment. When I got there, yes, she had left - I checked the room, bathroom and kitchen - I couldn't believe she left so fast. Where has she gone? Why would she leave in such a hurry? As I search for possible answers, I suddenly saw a note she left on the kitchen counter which reads.

"I cannot imagine my life without Bobby, so I will be taking some time for myself. You'll find true love Liana but with me around it will be difficult. Please don't worry, I'll be okay." Love Peaches.

I hold my lips tightly while exhaling intensely as I reach for my phone. I called her about a million times but no answer. I'm trying to think - pacing back and forth, I remembered Robert and immediately called him to find out anything I could about Peaches whereabouts. Robert didn't answer but I decided to give her a few hours at least or a day then try calling her again. I was afraid the letter means something, maybe a suicide note or she's been taken - I can't ignore my mind begging for answers I don't have. Should I call the police? - I asked myself, nibbling my nails.

Exhaling and bracing forward towards the kitchen window, Danny called, "Hi Liana, are you okay?"

"No I'm not Peaches is gone and she's not answering her phone, I came home and saw a note she left but I'm just scared she might not be okay"

"Liana it's okay I'm sure she will be fine, try to calm down."

"Danny I'm so worried I don't know what to do right now"

"Liana I'll be there in a few okay"

"Sure Danny I'll be here"

Danny came, and we tried to call everybody we knew would be able to provide some information about Peaches; just like an interview session, we tried not to alarm or get anyone worried, so we made up a story that we were trying to find out about all the friends she contacts, a few just to plan a surprise party for her and invite all her close friends.

I asked Danny to stay with me for the night as I was not comfortable staying home alone, I fixed a nice spot on my sofa for him as I didn't trust myself enough to invite him in my bed. He seems to be the perfect gentleman but he's not a threat - I am. In my mind I thought he would offer himself to stay but instead, I did, and he never tried touching or kissing me. I was impressed but wanted just a little bit of him. Laying in my room, I wanted to invite him to hold me and cuddle to sleep. So, I went to talk to him for a while and did just that. His body felt like a large pillow with extra cushions. All I wanted to do was kiss his lips and climb on top of him while he squeezed my paired posteriors, navigating his warm lips on my firm breast as I yelled his name in pleasure.

Liana are you okay? Danny shook me awake, "Yes yes I'm okay Danny. What's wrong?"

"You were moaning in your sleep and called my name."

I looked up at him embarrass "Oh snap Danny I'm so sorry I might have been dreaming I don't know".

It's okay Liana, get some rest I'm right here".

I couldn't believe I had fallen asleep so quickly and to make matters worse, he heard me moaning, if only he knew that I'm suffocating, not touching him I'm sure he wouldn't hesitate to make love to me if I just give a strong hint. Should I tell him I really wanted him? Damn I should take a cold shower first I'm horny as hell! Suddenly I got up and went to the bathroom and placed a cold towel on my love nest for a few minutes then ventured in the kitchen and poured myself a glass a wine - definitely defeating the purpose of phase one but what the heck - let's see if a boy can take a hint! As I swallowed it all, Danny came to the kitchen.

"Liana, what's wrong? Are you okay?" Does my presence here make you uncomfortable? I can leave if you want"

"No Danny no, it's not you; please stay. Let's go back to bed I'm sorry I just felt like having a glass of wine. I'm okay".

Okay let's go, I know you miss Peaches. I'm sure she's okay. He hugged me and we both walked back to the bedroom. I didn't want to seem desperate and initiate sexual contact so I turned away from him as I hugged my pillow and dream of what would have been a spectacular night. By morning he was already awake and ready to leave as we both agreed on the continuous search for Peaches. The moments of her found a thoughtful place in my mind as reflections of her life and our time together deteriorated me.

On day three (3) we went to the police station to make a missing person report, but based on the note she left, the officers advised that it was completely necessary to do so and of course, if she does show up we should take her to the station to gather a statement so as to close the case I guess. They questioned the handwriting and wanted to know if I'm sure it's hers, I felt like I was being interrogated since she was staying with me and I was the last person she spoke with. Understanding police protocols is almost impossible so I cooperated with them and left for work, hoping that Peaches was okay.

The following week I received a call from an unknown number, I looked at the phone and put it away. Thirty minutes later another call so I answered, "who is this?" Sternly. Hi Liana, it's Peaches, how are you?"

"Peaches, is that really you?" I asked with sudden fright holding my chest and providing my full attention as I listened keenly to her voice, analyzing any fear of discomfort.

Liana it's me I'm just calling to let you know I'm okay all I needed was time alone to gather my thoughts".

"That's fine, Peaches once you're okay, I'm happy".

We talked for a few minutes, hoping she would either come home or advice on her location, but the conversation ended abruptly as I tried to find out where she is. Nevertheless, I was happy she was alive and well. As the call ended, I kept thinking about her tone on the phone it sounded happy as if she has found love. The thought suffocated me as I dialed Danny's number to tell him the good news. He was elated and requested my presence for dinner. This time I accepted his invitation as it was a relief hearing from Peaches. He arrived at about 6:15 pm, with a double knock on the door. I opened it to a handsome man dressed in a white button front shirt with long sleeve cuffed navy-blue jacket and a black pants with matching shoes. His hand hidden behind him as he slowly smiled with a bouquet of roses. "They are beautiful," I smiled upon receiving them "I'll put these in water, and then we can go". As I walked away, he pulled me close to his chest and kissed me passionately removing some of my lipstick.

"Liana, you are so beautiful, sexy, and smart. I'm happy to be a part of your life. I smiled, rubbed his cheek, and went to put the flowers in water. Then we left.

At dinner, he ordered shrimp scampi pasta, and I had shrimp Alfredo with a glass of white wine sauvignon blanc and for dessert a slice each of chocolate strawberry cheesecake. As he devoured his meal, I admired Danny's facial expressions and how handsome he looks when eating, his smile exposing is perfectly arranged teeth and dimples. "What is it, Liana you've been looking at me for the longest while?" I'm sorry, was it that obvious?" I said with a grin. He shook his head and said "Its fine I'm beginning to think you enjoy my company." Flirtatiously I smiled "of course I do."

After dinner, we went home and I asked that he stay for a while, where we laughed and talked about the silly things we do at work and how I responded to him after countless invites to dinner - mocking my tone of voice. Feeling embarrassed, I covered my face and apologized, laughing. We didn't realize it was so late, it was almost midnight, so he reminded me he's not officially my boyfriend yet, so he'll be leaving. I have started to developed a strong emotion towards him, feeling for him, robbing myself of some good lovemaking, maybe the best I will ever have so this time I initiated a kiss, I climbed over him on the sofa and demanded it as we intensely exchanged the taste of saliva, feeling his hard rock seeking an escape route as it raised aggressively meeting my warmth beneath. He grabbed my waist and pulled me closer, gripping my hair to maintain a perfect pace as the adrenaline stimulated the organs and our bodies responded sexually, attending to my overdue desires. I moaned at every touch of his cold lips and warm breath as it shadowed my neck, igniting the craving of his shaft to penetrate my love nest. We hesitated at a pause of a kiss, and our eyes answered as we continued removing our clothes. I wanted him so bad, I would kiss him all night. I wanted him to just make love to me, please me the right way - taking control of my body and mind, he periodically spanked and gripped my gluteus maximus playing domino at every touch and teased my ears and neck with his tongue. I moaned with pleasure as I tried to put up resistance when he attempted to cup my breast and insert his finger beneath.

"Danny please I don't think we should do this" I stuttered. Kissing my breast and stomach, he then removed my laced Victoria Secret thong and, spread my legs and covered her with his mouth using his tongue to stimulate my clitoris. "Are you sure you want me to stop Liana?" breathing intensely I begged him not to stop holding his head in a firm position and gripping my nipples anxious to climax. He channeled his lips to my neck and lips and slowly penetrates me with his manhood, "oh fuck", he said slowly entering me with caution as his pace deepened reminding me that he's always visualize this moment and it's more than he imagined it would be. Without hesitation, he removed his well erected shaft as he rushed towards my love nest kissing her with his cold lips and devouring her juices. He turned me on my knees and enter from behind thrusting deep and fast, spanking my curved gluts, making a rhythmic sound as he yelled, reaching a climax. We smiled and kissed each other, astonished about our intercourse as his thick muscles captivated my body embracing tightly, breathing heavily until he was fully relaxed, he slowly pulled away and went to the shower. Laying there I urge for another round, so I went to join him. Where we kissed fervidly as I turned his back towards the warm flow of water and kneeled in front of him, tasting his shaft as I stared into his eyes, making movements with my tongue, exposing my throat as his facial expression changes, indicating moments of pleasure. We changed position as I enjoyed him once more from behind alternately tasting my juice from his manhood as it hardened making my inner core stretched as he stroked uncontrollably, my moaning increased "oh yes, yes Danny don't stop, right there" he was giving me every inch of him and I wasn't refusing anything but begged him for more.

In the end the feeling was bittersweet, we were exhausted and ready to hit the sack. We cuddled as he whispered, "you are truly a remarkable person and I would love to enjoy every bit of you". We smiled and slept the rest of the morning.

CONFESSIONS AND CONFRONTATIONS

Phone rang and I was awakened from my sleep, I glanced at the clock and it was 8:25am. The caller ID displayed Bev. Danny was still asleep, so I walked to the kitchen where I answered, "Hi Bev what's up?" She paused and asked, "Hi Liana is this a bad time I really need to talk to you?"

"No Liana it's not. Are you okay?" She was sobbing and sounded congested.

"I'll be there shortly okay" she said as she ended the call. Surprisingly I wanted to keep my affair with Danny confidential until we decided it's a "go". But since she sounded she needed a friend I just hope Danny is in no rush to leave and will stay quiet until she's gone. I wouldn't want to create another story in her head or a confirmation of a relationship that isn't.

I went to the bedroom and Danny was still asleep so I took some fruits and juice and left it on the bedside table with a note that reads "Bev will be here to talk not sure when she's leaving so stay put, text me if you need anything, Love Liana."

I sat in the kitchen and wait for her while I made some pancakes and eggs and coffee for myself and hot chocolate for her. I heard her drive in, and I went to hug her as she disembarked from her vehicle. "I made breakfast, so let's eat," I announced excitedly. "You seem to be in a good mood, Liana, is everything okay?" I smiled at her and said, "Of course I am Bev why wouldn't I be, don't worry about me hon, I'm fine?" she sat at the table and told me that Thomas is having an affair - "Bev, how do you know that he is, did someone tell you?"

"No Liana, I found out on my own, let me tell you what happened so Thomas came by over the weekend, when he arrived, I could feel his energy of sadness and guilt. I reached out to hug and kiss him, and he turned away and asked, "Are you okay?" Watching him walk away, I asked, "I'm fine honey are you okay?" He avoided the question and with a taunted tone he asked, "did you cook?" Liana I was now convinced something happened, and he decided to take it home, I wasn't in the mood to argue so I continued to ask questions"

"So what did you do Bev?" I asked worriedly.

Liana to be honest I answered, "yes I cooked" and went to the kitchen, took the food from the refrigerator and shared a portion for him, placed it in the microwave. "Thomas what's wrong?" "nothing" he yelled I had a bad day at work okay so please stop asking"

"You don't need to shout, Thomas I'm right here and I'm just concern okay, I'm sorry about your day at work, enjoy your dinner I'm going to bed"

Bev broke down in tears, as he finished her breakfast and ask for a bottle of water. "Liana I love Thomas so much, he proposed to me and we'll be getting married in a few months and he's pulling away from me I don't understand."

I was skipping through the channels on the television when I heard his phone ring and he answered and said "I can't talk right now, and please don't call me again unless I do" then terminated the call and put the remaining food in the microwave, went to the shower where he stayed for less than ten minutes and usually he would sleep in his boxers but this time he was fully clothed. "Who was that on the phone?" I asked he pulled the sheet and said "No one, good night."

I wasn't satisfied with that answer, so I provoked him until he turned around and hugged me "I'm sorry about earlier, okay, today was just not my day." he kissed me and shoved his hand under my lingerie and filled my love nest with two fingers. While he kissed me, I tried to ask him again who was on the phone, but he kept saying "No one" as he kissed my weakest spots to distract me. He took control and I was defeated, allowing myself to moan and groan at his inserts and deep penetrations. He held my neck tighter than usual and, increased his strokes and gripped my waist with his hand holding me firmly in place as I choked requiring the ability to breathe, he stopped

131

and turned me to the side quickly while stroking faster than ever. It was so good I didn't want him to stop but it was my first-time experiencing sex with Thomas so aggressive.

Liana I was moaning and listening to the sound of each stroke mixed with my orgasms. It felt like hammer connected to nail piercing through a wall. They were solid strokes and I could feel his breath on the back of my neck, searching for the perfect spot in my intact walls to trigger off an ejaculation. In time he was out of breath releasing his fully loaded secretion in my love nest. We went and showered together and enjoyed an intimate moment kissing and tasting our orgasms before getting refreshed and prepped for bed. He whispered in my ear "I love you Bev and appreciate all you do, I'm lucky to have you" he stared at me and squeeze my body while kissing me passionately as we hugged and slept peacefully.

Next morning, I woke up and I spotted a mark on his neck it looked like what we would refer to as a "hickey," which happens due to constant sucking at one area preventing the flow of blood. I shook him and woke him from his sleep "good morning babe" he turned and kissed my cheek. "I have a question Babe" I said to him, he looked at me and ask "you want more sex like last night? He smiled "No that's not it" and smiled and said, "what's that on your neck?"

"On my neck?" He asked astonished

"Yes Thomas on your neck!" He got up and rushed to the mirror in the Chester draw and turned towards me saying "This here you're talking?" Pointing at the area, he asked, so you don't remember doing this?" Looking at me with a raised eyebrow.

"Thomas, I didn't do that." I looked at him trying to be calm. "No, no, no" he said, "what are you implying Bev, that I'm having an affair or I'm fucking someone else, and they put a hickey on me?"

"Stop yelling okay, please, I'm just asking why there is a hickey at your neck, can you please explain to me why?

He raised his voice higher, trying to convince me I was the one who put it there. All I did was went to the washroom and sat on the floor and cried. He was lying to my face. No wonder he was so aggressive. He thought I wouldn't remember anything; he knew it was there. Telling the truth would be so much better.

I washed my face and accepted his answers. I proceeded to do laundry, so I took his clothes and check his pockets as usual before I put them to soak. I found a used pack of condom in his back pants pocket. Now I'm convinced he's cheating, there's no way he could lie his way through - this time I had something more I had evidence I said to myself. We are about to get married and if this what he wants he need to at least be honest. I felt warm betrayal and disrespected since he could cover it up so well. I went to the bedroom and told him to get up we needed to talk, and I needed the truth. But another barrier - seems to be the hardest thing yet. He yelled "leave me alone Bev, please!" He stormed in the bathroom and slammed the door shut."

"Thomas, Thomas please open the door, please just talk to me" I knocked and knocked and no answer. I could hear him brushing his teeth and washing his face. I broke down in tears "why would you do this to me?" I cried sitting at the door hoping he would open it and talk to me.

He suddenly opened the door and sat with me "what is it, why are you crying?" So I showed him the used condom I found and he took a deep breath and stared at me.

"Do you want the truth?"

"Yes I do, please" I said to him

"Okay, so I just needed something different, and I know you wouldn't want that, so I did so with a friend"

"What was it? Why couldn't you say something to me first to see if I would?"

"It's having the opportunity to do deep-throat fucking and restraints with another friend so basically it was a threesome okay"

"Is this something you will continue to do Thomas?"

"No, I just wanted to do that before we exchange vows okay? I'm sorry you had to find out this way"

"At this point you need to figure out what you want, Thomas, we are about to get married, and you're messing around and can't even cover your tracks" if this is what you want I'm sorry I can't marry you" relationships are built on trust and right now that's slowly drifting away"

"Bev I'm sorry it won't happen again I promise"

Liana my eyes were overflowing with tears, I had no idea what to say to him but explained how hurt I was and I'll need time to digest all he's told me.

"Bev, honey, take it easy I know you love him but it's up to you if you want to meet his desires, do you believe that you will not do it again?

Liana I'm confused right now, I don't know what he will do and once he's not committed the wedding is off.

Beverly was extremely nonchalant, and I was unable to provide her with an answer. I sighed and took a deep breath and responded, communication, loyalty, and trust are important factors to a successful relationship. In your case, Bev, Thomas needs to understand what your limits are and make your demands if he truly loves you, he will see the need to change and in return love you endlessly without causing any discomfort or pain.

It's not that easy, Liana, I know you mean well but, I can't continue like this, what I'm I supposed to do now?"

Listen to me, Beverly, you can do this. In the future, find a location that will allow him to be honest and open and advise on what is bothering him and what his preferences are. Sometimes, we fail to provide an environment suitable for men to express themselves. Listen to his views and discuss the "whys" in order to conclude his sexual

138

preferences. Try not to cancel all the opinions he has but improvise and illustrate how both can achieve his interest in a different way.

MOMENTS OF WEAKNESS

As Bev listened, she occasionally advised that she would try that route and hoped she's able to accomplish a way to overcome Thomas's new venture and sexual desires. She sounded confident but was hesitant about the effect that method will have on their relationship, and it might not work.

Soon, a message came on my phone, it was Danny he wanted to make a few calls and run some errands. "Bev, can you excuse me in just a second

I'll be right back." I took my phone and walked towards the room "sure, Liana no problem."

I opened the door quickly and closed slowly behind. Danny was already behind the door, "hey I'm sorry she will be gone soon." he kissed my lips and neck wanting me as much as I wanted him but I reminded him Bev is just outside the door "I'll be quick" he said. "Danny no, please don't" I was gasping for breath as he kneeled between my legs enjoying my juices as he lifts my body and carefully inserts his manhood ensuring she fits perfectly before changing the pace.

"Liana, is everything alright?" Bev knocked at the door, "yes Bev I'm fine. I'll be out in a minute" Danny placed me on the atman on my knees and was pounding like no tomorrow. I gripped the edge of the sheet and sucked his fingers as we both climaxed - it was a quickie! Felt so good I was weakened hoping Beverly would just relax and trust

141

I'll be there shortly, but I was wrong. She pushed the door opened and discovered Danny and I naked after a short sex, smiling.

"Liana and Danny, oh wow, you've been here the whole time?" Why didn't you tell me Liana?"

Bev, I wanted to, but since you needed me as a friend to listen to you, I couldn't burden you with this!"

"So, how long has this been going on?"

"Not long, Bev, we just don't know where this is going yet.

Danny asked that she turned away while we get dressed and yes the questions continued.

"So you couldn't wait until I leave to finish the sex, wow you guys are just unbelievable!"

Bev was laughing and I felt relief she was, as I was afraid she would be uncomfortable, but she was happy that I finally got some good sex.

Danny kissed my forehead and left. "I'll see you later okay?"

"Are you coming back?" I asked he smiled. "Do you want me to?"

"I'll think about it!" I responded, kissing him as he walked towards his car. "I'll take that as a yes." Bye ladies," he waved and drove away.

"Liana, you are a naughty girl, I thought we were best friends, we shared everything. How was it?"

"Bev come on not now"

"Yes, right now please tell me how it was?" I couldn't deny her innocent face of the truth so I said "It was amazing, I enjoyed every bit of it, and feels like I want more, too."

"Damn Liana, I'm happy for you girl, but I thought you said you wouldn't want to settle with a guy that is divorced and with kids, how will you work that out?

Shaking my head, I answered "Bev I'm not sure if this is what I want, I'm not settling, I'm just having fun, if he's the guy for me I just have to deal with it but I highly doubt it though"

We both laughed and said, "Enjoying the ride" I took a deep breath and asked her "will you be okay handling your situation at home?"

"Yea I think I will Liana, I appreciate it; thanks a lot"

"Pray about it Bev you'll be fine"

"yea I will, I'm going back home now, thanks for your hospitality"

Anytime Bev, anytime.

Danny called later that night and was on his way to see me when he caught a flat tire. Such a disappointment, all I wanted to do was head out there to be with him but instead, I stayed with him on the phone until the tow truck came. Reminiscing on earlier my body wanted to invite myself to his place.

I needed his touch, the feeling of his breath on my skin, and his soft kisses. "Stay calm," I reminded myself. I didn't want to seem desperate; I needed to be in control of my emotions.

"Liana, do you want to come get me at my place or stay with me tonight?" I was afraid he would ask this question.

"Danny, it's fine honey it's late and I'm sure you're exhausted from your errands today. Tomorrow will be a better day for you."

"Ok Liana, sounds like a plan. I'm going to shower and get some rest we'll talk tomorrow"

As the week progresses my thoughts ventured beyond my experiences and many observations seen questioning my ability to love and be loyal, happiness is my goal and having a partner that shares my views of being spontaneous and fun is an important attribute. All considerable moments took an eruptive path in my mind examining each to surrender fully to what I have been yearning for. A better life and a consistent romantic relationship. I took a walk down memory lane and reflect on all my encounters with families and friends who have experienced a monogamy partnership. In a flash, I concluded what I needed to do I need to be a resilient attacker and make new decisions new paths and execute all with a positive attitude. Gathering my thoughts, I was interrupted by a phone call. It was Peaches.

Hi Liana how are things with you?"

"I'm good, Peaches; when are you coming home?"

"I'm sorry Li I need more time plus I'm dating someone and I feel free and happy so I'm taking it slow and trying to find myself."

"Peaches, please be careful. Bobby has friends all over, and they might be looking for you."

"Liana I'm fine he can look all he wants I'm not going back to him; don't worry I'll be fine"

"So when will I get to meet this new partner?"

"At Bev's wedding, I'm still invited so I guess I'll see you then?"

"Peaches, that's months away. Please let me see you before that time, I just want to know you're okay"

"Liana I'm fine, I'll see you soon. I love you. Bye baby"

She hung up on me simply because I ask too much questions "damn, I wonder where she is and who she's dating?"

"Omg I can't keep up with all this." life is funny you know, I have all these people coming to me with their problems and I have to pray about mine. No one wants to listen to me, but I should listen to them, oh well I guess that's my purpose"

I was curious to find out what her new lifestyle journey is taking her and hoped to intervene and provide guidance to avoid a disaster.

Suddenly I heard a knock on the door, "who is it?" "Hi Liana, it's Danny - I was surprised as I didn't receive a call or text. I slowly opened the door and ask, "hey, what are you doing here?"

"I'm sorry I showed up unannounced, but I texted and called and didn't receive an answer, so I got worried," Danny explained.

"Oh, I'm sorry, I was on a call with Peaches, come in, come in and do you want something to drink or eat?"

"yea sure, I'd like a cup of coffee."

Danny was very supportive and maybe the person who would be good for me, but I can't seem to open my thoughts and heart to him. "Liana," he whispered. "Can I get some of you right now, right here in the kitchen, on this counter?

He scooped me from the floor and placed me on the counter, nibbling on my breast and searching for an opening to my love nest.

"Danny wait, please I think we need to talk"

"Yea we do baby, I hope we are together now Liana, not because we have sex but I can see it in your eyes that you want this, even when we're making love I can feel it"

"Yes Danny I want this but I'm just afraid but yes we're official."

We smiled and a steamy lip-sharing continuous renaissance developed capturing both body into a singular bond securing a therapeutic sexuality, engulfed into a romantic paradise.

We then switched to the sofa sitting on top his manhood, making him moan and groan as I contracted my love nest, gripping him with every move, deepening and rotating my waist slowly. "Oh, fuck Liana, if you keep doing that I will explode," I stared in his eyes "no baby please don't, I want more of you". He didn't want to stop so he suddenly took me walking to the bedroom wrapped around his waist, placed me against the wall, and slipped one finger inside, making his way deeper as he reaches for my G-spot. His tongue covered my nipples as he gently muscled around both breasts taking turns while caressing and stroking my love nest. I moaned loudly, gripping his body and stabilizing his every moment of pleasure. As he lay on the bed and removed his shirt, I quickly tuned my stereo to a song by 'H.E.R - I want to love you in every kind of way' I lay flat on my back with my legs wide open, massaging my thighs as I await Danny's inconsiderably passion for love. He slowly crept over my well-framed body and kissed each area, slowly inserting his finger once more repeatedly and allowing me to taste her, preparing for an entry into my warm, wet, desirable oven of pleasure where his hard, enlarged, dark chocolate shaft would find existence.

His gentle touch and warm mouth create shock waves through me, awakening my inner cravings for sex. His perfectly shaped lips celebrate with my mouth below as he deepens each stroke with his tongue inside to taste my every flow of orgasm. My legs lift above his shoulder as he inserts his well hard shaft deep within. My body trembles, receiving him with his repeated motion wave strokes. We became one as I grabbed his gluts into position and kissed his neck ferociously, and used my nails to create a tingling sensation over his back, squeezing and screaming, "Danny, fuck me harder, please?" I begged as he added an extra speed, increasing his pace, anxious to reach the pinnacle of our romance. He gripped my waist and yelled, "I'm coming baby, oh shit, I'm coming" almost inseparable, our lifeless bodies found comfort and fell asleep.

A New Day's Promise

The rays of the sunlight entered my bedroom opening our eyes to a beautiful day. As I turned and smile at Danny's handsome face in my bed, I couldn't resist captivating a personal photo in my cerebellum saved for days when his presence is needed but unknown. I went to the bathroom and looked at myself in the mirror, reflecting on our enjoyment and wondering why we hadn't synchronized before? I washed my face, doing my regular early morning routine when Danny walked in and held me from behind and stared at us in the mirror and said "we look good together, don't we babe" I smiled at him and agreed. "Are you okay?" He said I'm going to shower and go to work"

"Yea I'm okay just bruised from last night. I'm staying home today"

"I'm so bruised Liana I guess we need to take a break this morning" every time I see you, I want you more and more I'm like a rabbit seeking refuge in your nest. He laughed as we showered together and wash each other's back, and have some play time excluding sex.

I made his favorite breakfast: scrambled eggs, toast bread spread with pancake syrup, diced sausage fried with baked beans and coffee with orange juice. We sat at the table smiling at each other like high school love birds being entertained by our own story discussing our romantic entanglements we decided to take it slow with consistency. After breakfast he left for work and I got dressed to run some errands before my late afternoon shift.

Later that day a call was received from Constable Rose at the Police Station advising that he's calling on behalf of Brandon "Bobby" Stone, who is requesting some clothing items and food. The officer continued providing numerous restrictions against items e.g. no lace in shoes or can bring a pair of sandals for him; only a white bar soap should be used by Bobby and toothpaste should be poured in a clear plastic bag. He further advised of the visiting hours and times and that proper identification is needed for entry.

Receiving that phone call traumatized me and I was forced to call Crystal. I didn't have her number, so I decided to reach out to Robert.

"Hi Robert, how are you?"

"I'm good Liana; what's up?"

"I'm doing well, Rob. I need your help with something do you have a number for Crystal? I need to talk to her?"

"Yea I do just a second,"

I rang her phone twice, but no answer, so I left a message requesting an urgent call back. Why was Bobby reaching out to me? I didn't remember he was still locked up, and of course, I wouldn't expect me of all people to be on his lips since I was the one who took Peaches to his apartment to speak with him. What happen to his relationship with Crystal? Why not call her? The thought of ignoring the officer's call was most favorable for me, but somehow, I felt insensitive proceeding with what I agreed on. So, I waited for something else to change by mind, which will be suitable, and my conscience will be cleared. About 6 clock in the afternoon, Crystal called.

"Hello Crystal, this is Liana, how are you?"

"Hey Liana I'm well, how can I help?"

"Have you heard from Bobby or went to visit?"

"No, I haven't."

"Crystal, come on, why not?

"Why are you asking Liana?"

"He has called me requesting some stuffs so I figured the police has tried calling you and was unsuccessful so they called me instead, I just thought that since you're pregnant you'd go instead to see him please".

"I had a miscarriage, Liana, I made a mistake and now it's over, I'm sorry I can't help you,"

"Wait, wait please, Crystal I'm sorry to hear that but why would you not want to see him after everything you both have been through together?"

"I can't bring a child into this unhealthy relationship with a father who is in love with another woman, so I'm moving on. I'm sorry, Liana, I have to go, bye."

Before I could say another word, she was gone. This is disappointing - why would you break up a relationship just to break up again? I'm confused about her decision, but it's hers to make. Who I'm I to judge?

"What should I do? What should I do?" Then I figured I should call Robert once more and ask for some clothes; he should know where Bobby's belongings are, and I'll take them - with a heavy heart, I decided to go. Later that afternoon, Robert brought the items I had asked for.

"Robert, I really appreciate this - thank you."

"Sure Liana, let me know if he needs anything else"

"Sure I will. What cologne are you wearing, it smells really good?"

"It's Juicy Couture"

"I love it - I bought Peaches one for her birthday. Have you heard from her at all?

"No, I ... I can't say I have. I'm sorry," he stuttered

"Okay well I'll let you know what happens tomorrow when I visit Bobby"

"Sure thing, thanks.... bye"

Upon arriving at the Police Station I was there at 6am with my identification card as requested.

The area was filled with a mixture of calm and angry families and close friends. As I sat, I realize I had left the most important thing - the food. So, I asked one of the Sergeant on site what the process is and was advised that they provide food at a cost so I could do so. The Officers took us to the location where the items were placed in special containers and checked, and the person receiving them came forward.

Bobby looked at me and smiled "thank you" he whispered.

"I'm sorry" I lip signed as he acknowledged me saying "no don't worry about it, I have a court date next week and I should be out that time, my lawyer is making progress."

"Okay let me know if you need anything else, I left the food at home so I paid for food here for you okay, see you soon"

Bobby's eyes we're filled with tears, shaking his head and acknowledging my gesture of kindness, I felt hollow as I walked away, blaming myself for him being detained. When he's released, I'm sure he'll find out what Crystal did, and it will definitely destroy him, I hope Peaches will change her mind and give him a chance - after all, they've been together for years. I went in my car and wept bitterly. It bothers me that he's unhappy, and I can't help him, I didn't get a chance to hug him to tell him "I'm sorry" and I was just trying to help. In my mind I think he will try to get even, so I decided to set this straight as soon as he's released and I'm able to talk to him.

Feeling hopeless, I called Robert to update him on what Bobby had said but after a few times, no call was being received by that number. So, I decided to visit the community of Stonebrook in the parish of Trelawney, built with luxurious houses and mansions where my memory generates directions from previous visits. I remember being invited there a few years back when Peaches and Bobby began dating for a Christmas dinner and an after party. As I ventured into the area, I hoped I get the directions right my mind proceeded to navigate independently as I approached the gate. Luckily the same guard was there, so I was able to enter freely advising him of where I was going. Entering the driveway, I felt nervous, with my heart beating inconsistently in rhythm seeking composure as my eyes confirmed something spectacular. Peaches car was parked outside. Immediately I was tense. Horrible stories in movies I've watched devoured my mind wanting to call the police before I summoned him. I turned my engine off and listened for a moment and surprisingly, Peaches overwhelming laugh echoed throughout the air. I exit my vehicle and, walked up to the gate and introduce myself through the intercom. Robert came out looking to see if I was outside.

"What are you doing here Liana?"

"Please, I need to talk to you Robert I know Peaches is with you I heard her laughing. I won't say anything I promise, please"

A sudden buzz and the gate was opened, and I went inside. As I approached the entrance to the dining area and he looked at me and said, "be cool, don't say a word to upset her, please! I paused and took a deep breath and promised him I will listen to what they have to say. I could hear my own heartbeat drumming through my ear, and my mouth seem to just suddenly stop secreting saliva.

"Hi, Liana," She stuttered. Struggling to get the words out she hastily walked towards me and hugged me.

"I'm so sorry," she said.

"No, it's okay Peaches, are you okay?"

I quickly responded, touching her face and hands to ensure I was not seeing a ghost.

"Please sit," she said, "what's going on, and why are you here?" Robert offered us a drink and stood anticipating my reason for my unexpected visit. I told Peaches what Bobby had said and that he would be released soon hoping to see her and I wouldn't want for her to get hurt.

Robert is fearful that Bobby will try to interfere with their lives and would be devastated to see what he has done. I looked at them both and said, "what happened here?" Why and when did you both became attracted to each other?" Peaches stared at me, completely ignoring my questions and said "are you staying tonight we have plenty of rooms, and we have a lot to tell? "Oh my God! I responded I hope it's as much as I thought." as curious as I was, I had to agree on staying just to have a better understanding as to why Peaches got herself caught up in this situation. "I don't have the energy for this!" I thought. She took me to another section of the house and showed me where I would be sleeping, before I could secretly ask Peaches any questions, Robert came knocking, "settling in okay?" "Oh yes Robert, I think I'll be fine". He turned and left, and Peaches and I followed him to the living room and sat.

"So, Liana I know you have a lot of questions floating around in your head so we will tell you how it all started". Peaches glanced at Robert and continued. It all started a few years back when I found out Bobby was cheating. Robert would always be there to defuse the situation and provide comfort. One day I was at work and decided to leave early. I called Bobby just to see where he was so I could be alone to relax but he didn't answer. When I got to the apartment, I heard voices so instead of yelling his name indicating I'm home like

I use to. I quietly opened the door and followed where the sounds echoed from.

Liana I was in awe of what comes next. I walked in on Bobby with two girls in our bedroom having a threesome, the moment of fun in our shared apartment. The girls were in shock and began pulling for covering as Bobby yelled "What the fuck are you doing here?" He was as shock as I was as he walked towards me. "Peaches I don't know what to say, I'm sorry, I'm really sorry"

"Liana I was broken, my eyes were filled with tears, speechless, with nothing to say to him I did everything he wanted me to do. A threesome was the least I would do it, if he had ask, but to come home seeing him like that I was numb allover"

The girls were embarrassed and advised they will not continue and began to get dressed to leave. I watched and waited until they left to go ballistic on him, of course, I got a few 'blows,' but I surrendered after rushing to the bathroom to lock myself away from him. I called Robert, and he came within half an hour and spoke firmly to Bobby, but he wouldn't listen, talking about how he provides for me and gave me all I need, and I wouldn't let him breathe and have some fun. That night, I told Robert I'm coming to stay with him, but to be honest Liana, I didn't, I was afraid so I packed a few items I would need and stayed at a motel and tried crying and drinking myself to sleep. Robert called later that night to check on me and I told him where I was so without hesitation, he found his way to my location and stayed with me.

Seeing him making the effort to visit me no matter the consequences made me realize how much he cared and so I decided that my feelings for him changed to intimacy. We talked about all that happened and most of our personal life and struggles and we seem to share a common interest. All I thought about while listening to him was tasting his lips, and before we knew it - the taste was amazing. A quick feeling of comfort and love and reassurance. Liana, that was enough for me, so I held on to that feeling for a while and decided that we'll be there for each other no matter what the circumstances and ever since we have kept that promise.

As I sat there listening to their story my stomach hurts just the thought of what Bobby would think and what he would do if he finds out. Peaches stared at me with great hope of positivity and understanding towards their affair. But with a heavy heart I had to be honest - sometimes it's not what's best but in this case I guaranteed it was.

"Look guys" I stuttered, I know in the heat of the moment you weren't thinking, but now you are, and Bobby will not accept this union. He's dangerous and you both know that so my suggestion to you both is to end this while he's still in jail he'll be out by this weekend I'm sure.

Peaches and Robert looked at each other and said "Liana we appreciate your honesty and feedback, but we will remain this way. I'm sure Bobby will understand but if he doesn't, the law is there to protect us. I really don't think he will find her here" Robert explained.

"Robert" I said firmly, "if I can find her, I'm sure it's just a matter of time before he does. You know Bobby has a lot of connections, and he will not stop until she's found. I'm sure you won't be able to maintain your composure around him so you will become suspicious. Her car is parked outside for God knows how long, please, guys, wake up and think about this."

"So whatever you do, figure it out fast. This could get messy, and I really don't want that to happen so please come up with a better plan that what you both summed up to me. Be more vigilant since you both intend to ride and die to the end. Please figure out or someone will get hurt."

I could tell they both began to worry and see things from a different perspective, not to scare them but for them to embrace the impact of what's coming next. We went to bed and later that night I heard a whisper at the door "Liana, are you awake?" It was Peaches, I turned and looked at her as she closed the door and joined me in bed "I'm so confused now, I really love Robert but I'm more scare of what Bobby will do - just the thought of his reaction gives me a headache. I need your help nevertheless "can you be my eyes and ears on the street, and I'll figure out what to do?"

"You're my best friend, Peaches I'll try my best to do so"

"Thank you I owe you more" as she kissed my forehead and left.

RELATIONSHIP REALITIES

Next morning, I left and got dressed as quickly as I could for work. I was approached by my manager for our quarterly meeting to provide strategies that will be implemented going forward to increase production and improve network goals. I had a few ideas to share with the team and my manager was impressed. We decided to initiate a plan that includes combining out Top performers as subject matter experts to share best practices with our bottom outliers for two weeks after which a follow up will be done to analyze possible improvements or additional training.

After the meeting I went with Bev to the location of her wedding at Rose Hall Great House at the entrance of the mansion which for centuries entertains a host of tourist due to its legendary history of the White Witch of Rose Hall, it's culture, music and extraordinary panoramic view of the coast, a scenery of endless beautiful sea and sky; joined at the edge of the world. We went with the wedding planner Gloria and she provided a listing of decors and activities Bev requested with an additional exhibition at the end of the reception for family members. We selected the music for our march with the groomsmen, the cocktail recipe and the choice of wines. The invitation listing was challenging as we wanted to ensure our supportive friends and families were selected. Peaches and Bobby were on the list, but we decided to remove

Bobby and keep Peaches until further notice; her relationship with Robert may end soon however until that time comes, we'll discreetly disregard the thought.

As we sat and enjoyed a cup of lemon grass tea my mind demanded the outcome of a story Bev told about her future husband. I was curious so I decided to be nosy.

"Hey Bev what happened? Did Thomas agree to your terms and conditions?" I asked.

She looked at me and smiled. "I'm glad I called you that day Liana it helped us to be more open and honest with each other. So, he told me all about his supposedly short-term affair and he called and set up a dinner date with the side chick he was with and we spoke, and it helped me to understand the man I will be marrying. She has the 20% he wanted, and I now must work on improving that hidden sexuality and comfort for him. He has done all I've asked for to be happy with extra perks during the year. Extra special events for special anniversary such as birthdays, Valentine's Day and Christmas."

I felt relief listening to her and I promised to be her mentor or support in any way I could. "There's so much to do" Bev said. "I know, but at least you have me to help and your other bridesmaid - looking at her smiling I added. I'll delegate some task to find the best make-up artist and schedule date convenient to you for testing; also locate the top musicians, or maybe close depending on your budget. Videographers and photographers for your special day we have a few months before the wedding so we will coordinate and finalize specific dates and times when we will have a meeting to discuss progress and hiccups and find solutions where necessary.

Anxiously she said "here's an idea, Liana, on Friday I'll request to meet with all the bridal party" so I guess we can discuss our plan of action going further.

"That's more like it Bev. I'll be there!" We finished our meal and left for our homes. As I drove home my mind reflected on Peaches scavenging the feeling of guilt seemingly disturbing as I imagined the look on Bobby's face when he found out his betrayed and disappointed he would feel.

"Oh I hope I'm not there to see that" I murmured with my eyes filled with tears as I gazed in a distance; when I snapped back to reality I was speeding to the red light too fast. I immediately decelerate holding firmly to the steering wheel as the tires screeched and I made a quick glance staring in my rare view mirror. I noticed the appearance of black smoke ascending. Luckily, I wasn't being tailgated or else I could cause a massive traffic pile up or what we would call an accident due to drivers' negligence. As I came to a sudden stop the driver on my right yelled "watch where you are going lady and careful you kill us all, are you blind? Can't you see the red light?" Before I could answer the light changed to green and he drove off. My speed was 25mph on my way home.

"I need to hold someone tonight," I thought. Looking at James bedroom light in his window, I bit my lips and try to control my mind "no, no", shaking my head to erase the memories of our wild encounters, my phone rang and I quickly try to find my handbag on the back seat of my car to answer "why did I put this bag so far?" I yelled. It stopped ringing then once more in my hand this time. It was Danny "hey beautiful" he flirted, "hey Danny, what's up? I answered sounding dainty.

"I was thinking of coming by your place to spend the weekend together or you could come by my place, what you think?" He asked.

"I think that's a good idea Danny I would really like that. I just got home so I'm going to freshen up and wait for you okay?"

"Okay Angel" he charmed "I will be there within two hours." I parked properly and unpacked some items I had purchased earlier and went inside. I opened the windows and my door at the back to allow God's blessing of fresh air to enter my home, decreasing the level of heat that was settling inside. I didn't want to turn the air condition just the feeling of nature's best on my skin.

Anticipating Danny's arrival, I lay in my room watching a Jamaican Comedy called "Driva" I heard a knock on the door. "Danny is here already!" I whispered surprisingly as I ran towards the door and invited him in as he held my waist and firmly fixate his lips to mine, hugging me closely, "missed you much" he joked while pulling me closer and trying to find the passage for my love nest. I reached my hand down to the front of his pants and rubbed the already erected manhood in his unzipped pants. My body demands his shaft as I positioned myself to take it all in my mouth adding an additional feeling twisting my mouth and happy tongue in all directions while capturing Danny's facial expression from below. As I held his spongy sack of tissues, I imitate the action of pigeon picking continuously ensure he's fully erected and ready for entry. He held my hands and braced my back to the wall and carefully inserts his manhood slowly inside mourning at every stroke, reminding me how much I missed her. He was super romantic, hardening my nipples with his warm tongue and gripping them slowly, forcing my inner sexuality to penetrate his skin with my fingers and yell his name. He took me to the dining room and, pulled out a chair and lay me on my back as he pulled one leg apart and rest the other on his shoulder with continuous strokes until we both climaxed. My cravens seemingly increased, and I yearn for more, the feeling of Danny inside was magical, and I wanted him even more. A sofa break seemed like a great idea for resting so we relaxed, glued to each other as he gently rubbed his hand in my head, "you were amazing" he said.

"I enjoyed you too Danny, a lot more than I should" I complimented "but where do we go from here? I don't want to get hurt and I want to know that if we plan to start a relationship we both need to be ready, we had great sex, but our personality and expectations need to be discussed further.

He stared at me for a moment and said, "Liana I have been chasing you for months I think I made up my mind long ago and is waiting on you to decide what your decision will be."

Ignoring his question, I asked, "would you like something to eat?"

"Yes please, I'd like some hot chocolate if you don't mind." He replied.

Without hesitation I got up and went to the kitchen to get "my man" fed, as the thought came through my mind I giggled and wonder if this is what I really want? Is he really the guy for me? As I stood at the counter and rinse some utensils Danny came hugging me from behind, so I stopped but he demanded me to continue so I agreed. He then spread my legs and inserted his index finger, then got on his knees and place his head between my thighs. The feeling was extremely intense I removed my hand from the sink and held on to his head and mourned continuously until I almost hit my head on the counter. My body was shivering; loosing balance, Danny caught me and took me to the bedroom where I slept for almost two hours. I woke up and he was lying next to me, so I went and took a shower, came back, and kissed him on his forehead, and he rolled on his back.

"Did you have your tea, babe?" I asked as he smiled and nodded that he did since he put me to bed early. We both laugh. I climbed on top of him and played another of my hip-hop songs by Ciara, "Body Party" and danced like while we made love. I wanted to please him and show him what I could do romantically and for him to feel the sensation he drove through me, so I restricted him from touching me. I used his belt and tie his hands on the head of the bed and ensure I sat completely on his hard veined shaft and slowly moving to the rhythm of the song; teasing him with my tongue at his neck, ear and lips, simultaneously including his nipples. I rest my body on him from backward with my legs closed while enjoying his narrow ear canal making him a slave in my bed. Overpowering him with my tongue, he had goosebumps all over, trying to resist my intense affection. I continuously move my waistline back and forth as I lean forward and hold on to his knees, twerking my enlarged gluts, creating a vibration on the tip of his gland causing him to explode and flooded my love nest with his milky juices. He was struggling to be released so he could spank me but instead I kissed him and played with his body rubbing my tongue from his nipples to his waistline and navel. He begged me to stop and I felt so in control but a bit sorry for him - Knowing him I anticipate the punishment I'll get, so I did remove the restrains and cuddled to sleep in his muscular arms. For two weeks we spent every night together formulating a routine to fit our schedules. One evening I got home before Danny and before I could park properly James came over, greeted me at the door and assisted me out the car and kissed me unexpectedly; I immediately pushed him away but Danny drove up just in time to see it.

"James what have you done?" I yelled at him. "Please go" I begged.

"No" he said

"What's going on here?" Danny asked exiting his vehicle.

"Nothing" I responded quickly

"Well it surely didn't look like "nothing" to me" Liana! Danny said firmly.

"Who are you?" James stuttered, pointing at Danny.

"That's none of your business, if you know what's good for you, best you leave man" - Danny added pacing back and forth, anticipating an attack as James rushed over to him and throw a blow.

"Stop it, stop it guys!!" I yelled.

They were hitting each other, trampling my plants and denting my car. I ran next door and called James's dad, and he came and separated them, asking numerous questions that I surely couldn't answer but advise both of my one-night encounter with James and what he told me about his girlfriend. James was upset because I didn't tell him about Danny - in which I didn't think I was obligated to do, but shit happens! But I guess he felt a feeling of entitlement since we had sex and he felt jealous Danny had been staying at my apartment. His father grabbed him and took him away. Astonished and undecided as I was, I went with Danny to the living room. He didn't say anything but told me he's fine and went to the bathroom.

When he got out, he sat outside in the backyard. My hands shivered with nervousness as I slowly walked and sat beside him as he used a heating pad to cover the area he was hit. I began to explain my encounter with James, and he said with great anger "why didn't you tell me about him before?" "I'm sorry Danny, it's an old fling I didn't think was important" I responded sobbingly. "I didn't want you to know and I didn't think anything like this would happen."

All I was thinking about was that Danny will dismiss our relationship but instead he asked that I give him some time to process everything and speak to me after once he's in the right frame of mind to have a conversation about it again.

"Danny please don't leave," I begged, hugging him and apologizing over and over - kissing him on his face trying to get him calm to stay and talk about it. I wanted to know how he felt and how I can make things right. I became vulnerable using sex as an ammunition to defuse the situation.

In my mind I thought sex could sometimes help to create an atmosphere of comfort to conclude on common areas like this but I have learned the hard way it usually allows the person to feel good at that moment but when it's all gone they will remember what led to sex and the situation will become even more sensitive to normalize. We had great sex but after he was done, he didn't want me to touch him - he wanted only the satisfaction of an ejaculation and soon after told me he will be staying at his apartment that night. No matter how I pleaded, he decided to go so I let him be. Standing there like a lonely sailor I cried as I watched his brake lights faded.

My phone rang and I went hurriedly to see if Danny wanted to use this medium to express himself instead of face to face confrontation, but I was disappointed as it was James.

I decided not to answer, it was not the time to argue or be submissive, so I placed the phone on the table and ignored his calls and hoped he'd leave messages or a voicemail.

A heavy heart and a broken heart never seem to happen all at once, but a feeling of guilt lingers as I went inside and cried bitterly hoping that Danny got home safe as he rejected all my calls and left my messages unread.

"What have I done? How can I fix this?

"Liana, Liana please let's talk about this I'm sorry about what happened," James shouted from outside.

"Go away James!" I yelled.

"Why are you here, man?" I don't understand, you're the reason for her pain right now" a voice sounded like Danny was heard. I wiped my eyes and looked outside my window and there they were arguing but this time calmly, I guess.

I quickly opened the door and walked closer to the gate where they are standing.

"Go back inside Liana" Danny said

"Liana it's okay, I just want to talk to him a minute" James explained

"Please guys no fighting, talk if that's what you both will be doing, I'll be inside. Danny where's your car?

"It's on the other side of the scheme I'll go get it in a few"

I went back inside and closed the door, forcing my ears to listen I could hear them arguing intensely. Until they both agree that James was to never interfere in our lives again, and he surprisingly walked away.

He stopped in the middle of the street and said, "I can't promise you I won't continue to be her friend though, but I'll let you enjoy her all you want"

"Whatever man, just stay away. I'm warning you man" Danny said, walking towards the driveway.

As he entered the living room, he walked over to me sitting on the sofa, and stared for a few second. I love you, Liana and I really was hurt about what I saw but in order for me to forgive you, I wanted to see for myself the woman you are when I'm not around and now I know that you did not intentionally wanted to hurt me, and I want to be here with you tonight.

He kissed my lips gently and proceeded to the door. "I'm going to the car. Are you coming?"

"Yea sure, let me change really quick" I excitedly said.

Searching for something to tease him with for that night, I changed my underwear to a silk pink thong with beads around the waist and underneath to stimulate my love nest while walking and prepare her to receive him with a short cotton floral dress and my sandals.

"I'm ready, let's go babe"

189

We walked and talked about what we would do going forward and how honest we would try to be with each other, but I never wanted to talk about that. I just wanted to get to the car and make love to him. He surprised me, and I'm happy he came back.

"There is my baby," he yelled when he saw his car.

"You're crazy, but you need to name your car like I named mine okay."

"Liana listen, Dora is no name for a car, okay, you need to change that" he joked. We laughed and went inside but as he started the ignition, I was hungry to taste him while driving even if it's not for long but to feel like I have a stuffed mouth filled with candies for a few minutes – Oh I can't wait. So, without asking I reached over and rubbed my wet mouth on his pants and pulled his zipper down as his hard manhood demands exit. He helped to remove him so quick as I showered it with saliva making sloppy sounds that he reacted to moaning and begging me not to stop and holding my head deeper to cough with him still deep inside my throat. As we approached the driveway he quickly stopped in the middle of the road, and leaned his seat backward while allowing him to enjoy my sloppy blows. He was on cloud nine, shouting and yelling and I wasn't making it easy for him to relax. I did it just the way he liked it!

"You're bad, oh no Liana, You're a freak! He yelled I wanted him to explode, I wanted to taste all of him – Did I mentioned I was hungry? Yes, I did!

"Liana, Liana, baby, baby I'm come -in, yes I'm coming baby" Ohhhh, Ohhhhh fuck! Danny screamed like a baby while securing his manhood deep in my throat. I slowly removed all his milky juices as he held my face and kissed me deeply.

"You were amazing, how did I end up with a lady and a freak like you?" he praised, taking deep breaths as we continued home.

We parked and emerged from the vehicle slowly and went inside where he made river channels in my love nest stroking me from behind on the sofa arm until the river dried up. I never thought I could squirt so easily but the way he did it, sends temporary shockwaves to my thighs and dried my mouth. I kept on rehydrating at every climax. I feel so numb when I'm almost at the edge and then he just removed his manhood and rubbed my clitoris extremely fast and "voila!" the waters flooded the riverbanks. A unique release of undying romance that requires techniques and patience to achieve, but more importantly, an understanding partner who won't judge if something should happen, like the release of air/gas or what we call fart.

I know for sure some women have never climaxed before and it's all because our partners are not observant and skipped foreplay and romance and just get right into fucking or some may say 'stabbing of the meat'. If the stabbing should occur, I would want for my partner to listen to where I moan the most and in what position, and at what pace. Its more rewarding when we both achieve what lovemaking is all about – climax!

Suddenly my phone alarmed, and it was time to go to work. I hit the snooze button to give myself a few more minutes to sleep rubbing my warm body on Danny's back with my left hand, massaging his manhood for an early morning snack before showering and getting ready for work. Danny has a great sense of humor and enjoys making jokes about my friendship with Bev and Peaches totally opposite people but seem to play an important role in my life.

"Okay Danny enough of your jokes, that reminds me I need to call Peaches and I need to meet with Bev today for additional planning for the wedding.

We both got dressed and left in different directions. I decided to meet with Beverly first at a popular restaurant in Montego Bay, where we had some Chinese food. She ordered sweet and sour chicken with chicken fried rice and I ordered curry shrimp and white rice. I watched her as she seemed lost and signs of frustration covered her face.

"Bev are you okay? How are things with the wedding?"

"Liana, that's what I want to talk to you about, I'm not feeling happy anymore, and I just get the feeling that this is going to be a nightmare and maybe I should give ourselves more time. We are four months away and the plans are changing and I really don't know what to do"

"Bev, I just think that you're overly excited and stress at the same time and hoped that this day will turn out to be beautiful. Don't worry, everything will be okay." I'm right here to help you with all of this, why didn't you tell me?"

"I may have to make a few changes, Liana for the food and the additional list we created for old friends. We have decided, Thomas and I that we will only have one hundred and fifty people at the wedding, including ourselves. The package deal will cost us thousands less if we do not exceed that number. When we receive acceptance then we will know if there will be vacancy for the persons from the list we cancelled."

"Sounds like a great idea Bev. I'm glad Thomas is working hand in hand with you he seems very cooperative and excited to. But one thing I want to ask, will we be ordering the dresses, or will we all need to get a tailor?

195

"Oh I'm glad you mentioned that Liana, oh food is here. Thanks – looks delicious."

As we took turns sharing our food except for the chicken and shrimp as Bev is allergic to shell food and I'm just tired of eating chicken. We further discuss the dresses as she had some examples she would like for us to wear and we would order the sizes that fit us. She had to make the order that same weekend to have them delivered on time and to have time for any adjustments necessary.

"The colors Thomas and I agreed on would be midnight blue suits for males with burgundy ties and boutonniere, carefully matched men's brogue or oxford shoes since they are irresolute as to what would complement the entire outfit. The groom is what I'm concerned about however as he's marrying yours truly and I want him to stand out amongst the groomsmen so I thought about giving Thomas some ideas for himself but I would prefer if you find a way to do that for me Liana. My preference in his appearance on that day should be him wearing a derby or a cap toe and plain toe oxford or a Gucci loafers men's dress shoes or any popular brand that I enjoy wearing. I expect his beard to be carefully groomed and a haircut that will instantly seduce me and prepare me for the rest of the evening – I bet I'll be tired Liana. My brain is on fire right now, please tell me what you think?"

"Remember I told you women are attracted to different body parts on a man, yes, this is one of them, Bev outlining her preference to get sexually prepared for the bedroom." That was a thought that ran faster than I could remember in my head before I could give my opinion on her ideas.

"Bev, please honey don't get all worked up you're doing well, I admire how proactive you are ensuring the "T's" are all crossed and your "I's are dotted. You need to relax okay and breathe, everything will be okay." She felt better as I convinced her about every inch of her aligned preparation being on time and myself as an added support.

"So tell me Bev, what about us, do you have any ideas for our outfits and also yourself?"

"Yes, Yes, of course I do"

The bridesmaids will be beautifully dressed in burgundy mermaid dresses, exposing detailed body postures and curves, with all wearing the same hairstyles, accessories and comfortable shoes. The bouquets will have both colors and of course, I'll be dressed in my elegant beige and white off-the-shoulder laced dress, dominating the walkway with its train of stitched embroidery delicately designed to invite the ray of sun to smile making my entrance to my forever. I have picked out my shoes and second dress for evening wear, come, look at this Liana, what you think?"

She was the most exciting bride I've ever seen; the way she is able to describe the day in advance so deliciously it felt so real. To be honest, I felt a little jealous but shoved it off quickly, I want to get married but a long, hard pause on that current relationship I'm in so let's focus on Bev – I tried to get my mind in the moment of the wedding planning and to avoid distractions since Bev keeps repeating herself, cause I'm drifting away even when I'm looking at her and doing my verbal nods, I'm not hearing a thing! But then my brain helped with that transition and I was back to reality.

"Wow Bev this is awesome; you're going to be a beautiful bride"

"You really think so Liana? I'm so nervous."

"Don't be. You'll be fine, I'll be right by your side"

She looked at me with comfort and relaxation knowing that since we have been kids, we are like peas in a pod and on her special day I'll be by her side.

"So I guess we're all set for the clothing for the bridal party, right?"

"Yes Liana, we are, do you want to grab lunch?

"Sorry honey, I would love to be I have a meeting later that I need to prepare for, I'll call you later okay"

"Oh sure, Liana, it's fine I'll call you later for sure I have a few details we need to go over with the wedding planner and as usual you need to be there"

"You know I will Bev, catch you later"

I hurriedly went to the parking lot and drove off. I hate myself for lying to her about Peaches, and I don't know how to tell her that she's now living with Robert and seem happy. I had promised her to keep it a secret and travel there to see how she was doing after the meeting with Bev. Heading there, I was little uncomfortable as my shoes was too tight and since I had taken the car to the car wash I had removed my sandals that I enjoy driving with, so I decided to stop at my apartment and shower and relax for a while and dress in something more comfortable. As I drove into my driveway, I realize a car was parked on the opposite side of the road that I wasn't familiar with, so I stared for a while, opened my gate, and drove in.

In a flash the person walked up to my door, I looked up, and it was Bobby. "My God, what are you doing here, you almost give me a heart attack?" I yelled and stuttered at once as he smiled

"Liana, come on its me don't you recognize my car?" Where's Peaches I thought she was here I was coming to surprise her and to apologize,"

"Bobby, you're so crazy. Couldn't you call first?"

"No Liana, why would I call I told you it was a surprise? I'm really sorry I startled you, okay, please forgive me"

"Okay, okay Bobby, it's fine don't get all emotional on me. Peaches is not here, I'm sorry she left, did you check her apartment?"

"Why would she leave Liana, come on open the door I know she's here?"

"Bobby she's not here and I can't get to her phone I don't know where she is okay, I'm sorry?"

"What do you mean by that Liana? You of all people don't know where she is, hell no, I don't believe that! "

I was exhausted by the questions and didn't know what to say and was hoping he didn't ask too much, and I say the wrong thing to give him a hint that I'm lying to him. That will just make the situation even more complicated. Why do I get

202

myself caught in the middle of this complex relationship? My brain was on fire, and since he didn't believe that she wasn't home, I gladly opened the door for him to take a look.

I went to the refrigerator and poured myself a glass of water and add some ice cubes to quench my thirst real quick, I swallowed it so fast my brain froze.

"Do you want something to drink?"

"Yes please, do you have Hennessey or Vodka?"

"Yes I have both which do you want?"

"Hennessey on the rocks please," he responded making his way to the sofa and turned my television on to a movie channel.

"So Peaches has disappeared off the face of the earth, and her best friend is unaware of her whereabouts, I find that odd?" wouldn't you?" he stared at me from a distant, hoping that I would at least tell him something. But he wasn't going to interrogate me in my own place, so I quickly said, "Bobby, have you tried her cellphone?" look at this note, she left this the last day I saw her and I haven't heard from her since, so believe me when I tell you I don't know where she is"

He took a few sip from his drink and read the note while handing it back to me. "Okay, I guess she is hiding somewhere but if you do hear from her let her know I'm looking for her, and she should call me. Here's my new number". As he finally finished the drink, he placed the glass on the counter and left.

"Sorry to bother you, Liana, see you soon. I'll be watching you" pointing at me with his fingers.

"Bye, Bobby, if I hear anything, you'll be the first to know, I'm sorry I couldn't provide you with what you were looking for"

"It's fine Liana. Thanks again"

"Sure" I responded, standing at my doorway until he drove away once he's gone my first instinct was to call Peaches, I did but got voicemail. I tried Robert and the same thing happened. Where the hell can they be? I hope he took my advice and gotten rid of Peaches car because if that's not the case, Robert and Peaches are up for a great surprise. I decided not to venture to that location as I didn't want Bobby following me since he clearly state that he will be watching me. Perhaps this is a good sign I think Bobby should just move on and forgive his best friend for grabbing what seems to have fallen into his lap. What if she's pregnant or something, and to think of all that, I wonder what happen to Crystal if he visited her yet and heard about her miscarriage? He's probably not sure yet or else he would have mentioned it to me when he was here pondering and taunting me about his precious Peaches.

I waited for fifteen minutes and call her again and she answered.

"Liana where have you been?" she yelled

"Peaches you would not believe what happened to me just now. Bobby was here looking for you? I didn't want him following me there, so I changed my mind on coming"

"What! What do you mean he was there, at your apartment? He's crazy!' thanks for the heads up I'm going to tell Robert, just a second, Rob, Rob come here baby" she called out to Robert to tell him what I've told her.

Rob knew if Bobby showed up that's it for their relationship unless he has a plan. Bobby is unpredictable and will try to get Peaches back at all cost. He loves her and Robert knows that, but I think she should just tell him instead of him finding out. It's best to not make it more awkward. My interest lies with Peaches as she's caught between a rock and a hard place.

"Peaches, I think you should see him instead of hiding he'll find you and since it is in the arms of his best friend, he will be disappointed and angry and make things difficult for you"

"Liana I'm pregnant." I paused for a minute and responded; Peaches you are, what?"

"I don't know but it wasn't something we planned but it just happened okay. I don't plan to give that up Bobby will just need to understand".

"Are you going to call him? Just talk to him and see what happens instead of him hunting you."

"Liana I'll talk to him first by phone, and we'll take it from there, but I will do whatever I can to protect this baby. So Robert and I will discuss what we'll do going forward. I appreciate you looking out so much for us Liana, but can we finish this later honey"

"Of course Peaches anytime, bye".

Ending the call with her I became worried and anxious to hear what she has to say after calling Bobby to advise him of what chapter he is at in her life. No one knows what actions he will take when he realizes he's been betrayed. I'm concern and afraid but at the same time happy that she finally got what she has been waiting for, the feeling of motherhood and to experience this with someone who will be there for her and keep her safe. He may not be the love of her life and the person that she dreamt of but it's love and love come in different packages. Hers was already unwrapped and was waiting for her to collect it. She did and it was received joyfully. I'm convinced that she may only be able for a moment, but I pray she will overcome what is coming her way and will embrace it with her partner leaning on each other for strength and encouragement.

I reviewed the list I made of the person I wanted to be with forever and what my expectations are for him and I realize that most of the guys I've dated have reached at least 70 to 80 percent. So the question in my head signals; why I'm I still single; well, technically I'm dating but why I'm I not married then? I can't seem to find the answer but for sure my sub consciousness will reveal this when the time permits it to do so.

The times I spent with Robert and Peaches made me realize that sometimes we just need to take a leap of faith when falling in love. I strongly believe they were meant to be. Seeing the way, they communicate and speak to each other, especially when providing their opinion is a beautiful thing to see. They trust each other with decision-making most of the time but that works well, perhaps the best scenario I've seen in a perfect world – well who I'm I to judge?"

"Hey baby, how are you, I didn't know you were home?" Danny walked in and kiss me on the cheek.

"How was your day? I asked

"Definitely boring baby. I need a few new workers to cover the delivery department they are expanding and I'm a few guys short?"

"So who do you have in mind or do you plan to have an interview process set up with HR?"

"I have some applications. Maybe you can help me make a short list"

"Of course I can baby, let me see?"

As I took the paper and look at the applications, I realize Robert's credentials were amongst the listings. I did not know he was not working.

"Who are you talking about, honey?"

"Robert, Peaches new boyfriend"

"Wait, what, let me see that?" Danny took the papers and browsed through quickly. "Well I'll call him and give him a shot what do you think?"

"Yea I think you should"

"So why are you home I thought you were going to visit her today?"

"Yes, I was but after leaving Bev I came home, and you'll never believe who was here waiting?"

Danny suddenly stared up at me and said, "please save me the guessing and tell me James didn't come back here?"

"No baby it wasn't him, it was Bobby, he came here looking for Peaches."

"what did you do, are you okay, why didn't you call me?"

"Danny I'm okay, really I just told him that she's not here and I haven't heard from her so I presume he will be looking for her, so I called her and let her know"

In short Danny and I were concerned about Peaches and Robert and is aware of their histories together. Robert and Bobby have been friends for years and it would be devastating to know that this friendship would be destroyed by a female they both fell in love with. Peaches is one lucky woman to be chased by two great guys.

I felt jealous knowing Danny and I are taking things slow, we may have moved in together and seem to enjoy having awesome sex but sometimes I think we need to spice things up a bit he's always working and seems to take his work home sometimes, and request my help too so it takes away the time we need to bond and ignite the relationship as we should. Sometimes to be honest,

I feel like we are just friends with benefits – great benefits.

As we set aside the list for the workman he needed, we agree to call Robert first and offer him the job. He was super excited, moreover, to know he would be working with Danny at his company. He does merchandise where he delivers goods all over the island to several local supermarkets, bars and grills, corner shops and restaurants. It seems profitable and beneficial for him. Plus, we get to spend more time together and of course, with his daughter. I have not gotten a chance to meet her yet, but he insists that we wait as she is overly sensitive and he would not want to introduce her to different women until he has found the right one. I respect his opinion and would support his decision based on his daughter, a child's need should be taken into consideration when someone is deciding to start a new relationship and has been separated from a marriage or even a long-term relationship the child is already attached to – and never imagine that mommy and daddy would be separated and bringing a new partner to appreciate and respect. It is almost like us as adults having multiple relationships and when we end one, we are afraid to start over again and we make judgments about the person before we are deeply involved. It is the same reaction a child will portray after separation at a tender age / overall with both parents. It can be terrifying and cause the child to develops hate for whoever decides to be involved with that person.

So in a nutshell I prefer to take every precaution I can just to ensure Danny and I are ready and his daughter won't drive a nail between us as he claims his decision to move on will depend on his daughter's reaction – he will do whatever it takes to make her happy. No heart feelings to that I am extremely worried about his statement and that means his daughter could be a threat to our relationship. I have fallen for him so much I think I even Love him, but the thought of losing him is unbearable.

I never express myself to Bev about the relationship between Danny and I, and I think I should at least explain to her and get a decision, so I will not be heartbroken. Danny and I rarely talk about the future or where we will go from being common-law couples to becoming a married couple. Before we started dating, he always mentioned what he would do if he belonged to me. He always wanted us to go out on dates, text and call me all the time but living with him all that seem to be a joke. Nothing remains the same. His interest is with his daughter and his work. He has become my best friend, or some may say friend with benefit - oh here is a better one, he is my roommate. I was sitting in the bathroom laughing to myself and wondering why this is happening after months of courtship.

EMOTIONAL ROLLERCOASTER

As I showered and went back to the living area, I heard Danny talking to his daughter Brianna about school and her lessons, and upcoming events. He was so happy talking to her that not even my presence was a distraction. I felt jealous as I had longed to have conversations like those with him and to just feel him chasing me again. We are a bit distant and it seem I have become invisible in his eyes, but how can I rekindle the sparks we had lost. I have my second glass of wine while listening to his conversation - well not too much, but captured a few phrases. I was waiting for him to say 'goodbye' so I can have him for myself, tease him a little and make love to him the way we have done in the past. I became desperate and walked towards him sitting in the sofa, signaling my desire. He looked up and got up and, walked towards the bathroom, went inside and close the door.

Shockingly I thought I would be yelling at him but strokes of disappointment hit me all I did was went outside for a few taking deep breaths at a time to help me relax and prevent my body and mind from reacting to his gesture. As disappointed as I was, I went to bed and tried hard to sleep. As I lay there, I could hear the flow of water from the shower which I think helps to relax my mind to fully concentrate on sleeping, and of course, with the help of a small percentage of alcohol.

The alarm sound and it was 5 o'clock - Danny was not in bed. In my mind, I thought he didn't want to disturb me, so he slept in the sofa. But in my opinion, I think something is bothering him and he failed to acknowledge it or even talk to me about it. As I staggered to the bathroom to shower for work, I felt the need to speak with Danny about how I felt and also to have a mutual understanding of how we can move forward without feeling uncomfortable. He was tossing and turning as he was dreaming so I went close enough to talk to him.

"Hi Darling, how are you, did you sleep well?" whispering as I looked down on him. He looked disgruntled and unbothered as his eyes partially forced open to the sound of my seemingly sexy voice, but I demanded an answer for what happened the day before that led him to sleep in the sofa. He turned over and asked, "Is that important right now?"

"Yes, Danny it is, I just need an answer, is everything okay with Brianna? Why are you acting strange?"

"I'm not acting strange Liana, I just need to sleep right now so if you want to talk we can do that later, but not right now please." he was very stern with his decision towards me, I want to respect that so I went directly to the bedroom and got dressed for work. Upon leaving, I tried to signal that I was leaving but he didn't move from the way he was so I just left for work.

As I pulled up, I saw my Manager in the parking lot, I felted depressed seeing her since I have a weekly client call and a calibration session about my teams' performance and how they can improve but I have no clue what else to do, my mind was filled with thoughts about Danny and how foolish I am to have fallen in love with him. I blamed myself for not paying attention more towards his attitude at work or ask more questions about him. Why all this time he is single? There are so many girls at work that would be a fit for him but why hasn't he mentioned anything. I need to do more research and get some insight into him. He's not talking, so I need to do this by myself to get a better understanding. Maybe I should talk to his ex-wife if she would agree to see me. If I choose to venture further, I think that's best, but who can I get her contact information from?

This is indeed a setback for me today, I need to concentrate on my work to ensure I keep my job, support my team, and continue to exceed my expectations with my boss like I always do. I seem to keep thinking about others rather than myself - when will this end!

"Hey Liana, meeting is in ten minutes, please be ready" my manager mentioned as she swiftly congratulated the team on maintaining their performance; however was dissatisfied with their attendance. She insists that there will be strategies in place to change the pattern for absenteeism and lateness. The team was very attentive and promised to do better going forward. I encourage the group where I can; however, sometimes they have so many different stories that seem realistic, but consistency may increase the use of pen and paper and the use of ink. That is one of my favorite phrases they seem uncomfortable with when I raise my eyebrows and speak firmly.

At the meeting, I was asked about training used to close knowledge gaps and was introduced to a dynamic change in experience amongst the group. Clients were thrilled to hear the idea that will be implemented to boost performance and hopefully the added incentive will change the pattern of absenteeism. My Manager offer to have small competitions for agents that are consistent and for the most outstanding person for the month, they will be rewarded with a monetary incentive as a token of appreciation. This was an amazing suggestion and after highlighting the consistency and the change in performance for the outliers, she in tern acknowledged my dedication and strong leadership techniques to ensure network goals are met week over week.

I was surprised, I was able to maintain my composure during the meeting and confidently expressed my team's performance. My team was overwhelmed with the new strategies and agreed to work harder to maintain their scores and help to reduce my workload by issuing letters and reprimanding them for their incompetence. We decided to separate the team into two groups and assign Team Captains to each. These captains will track their team's performance or agents assigned to them and conduct one on one sessions once per week. Of course, the captains will need to maintain their own scores above their expectations but share these best practices with their team members. This tribal knowledge strategy will close knowledge gaps and increase performance. I was extremely excited to spearhead this approach and is thrill to see the outcome. As I explained this strategy to the other supervisors, some gravitated to the idea, but others seem delighted and inspired to achieve their goal and thought these strategies will be the answer.

Within two hours I was able to complete the calibration sessions with two groups of agents a mixture of top performances with the outliers that were present and get their feedback on some areas of opportunity. They were so elated to critique a few of their calls and to hear out loud the tone used based of questions asked by the customers and also the length of time they place the calls on hold. We have had so many issues with refreshing a hold where a two-minute hold time turns into five and ten minute. These areas will be monitored closely to ensure a reduction is achieved. Oh my I said to myself this team-building scenario gives me headaches and makes me hungry.

As soon as it was lunchtime, I tried calling Danny but no answer, I sent a text message and no reply. I began to get worried, so I reached out to Bev to really tell her how I feel. I dialed her extension and she was busy with her team, so we agree to meet after work. For my entire shift I kept calling and no answer, so I asked my team lead to stay with the team for the last hour and I went home early. I wanted to ensure he's okay, so I checked my apartment first and then drove to his. His car was not there, and he was not answering. I went home, showered and poured myself a glass of wine and lay on the sofa waiting for him. He never showed up and I slept until morning. Danny was still not home and no messages or miscalls from him. This is rather odd I imagined, my feelings were not taken into consideration here. How can you intentionally ghost someone you love and mean no harm?

My phone rang, it was Bev, Hi Liana, how are you? She sounded excited as she proceeded to tell me about her night with Thomas and how wonderful he has been these few days. I listened to as much as I can and tried to give my input towards her conversation. Some things sounded different in her great story so I thought I should ask a few questions.

"Bev, I heard you mentioned that Thomas went out with friends and stayed over. Is that right?"

"Yea Liana he did but it wasn't a big deal I spoke with him and he seem responsible, so I thought it was good for our relationship to have a night away from each other and spend the time with friends we know"

"Oh that seem like a healthy approach for your relationship once you both agree to that, I may try that for me and Danny and see what happens."

"Hey, I forgot to ask Liana, how are things with you and Danny, I haven't heard much since he resigned?"

I paused for a moment trying to find the right phrases and words to use just to get Bev's perspective and not her pitying me when I ask her questions about Danny and my current experiences with him, not to mention him staying out late and ignoring my calls and text messages. She is very emotional and sensitive so I wouldn't want to burden her with my relationship issues in a time like this when she is planning a wedding and depending on her maid of honor to help where my services are needed.

"I'm glad you asked Bev, things are okay with us, he's been such a sweetheart and support me emotionally" Those words fell from my lips shockingly, totally diverting from what I wanted to ask.

"Wow that's wonderful Liana, see, he was a great pick"

"Yea Bev, I couldn't agree with you more honey"

"So where is he now Liana? Is he at work?"

"Yea he is working early today, so he left already, you just missed him"

"Oh wow, I guess business is doing well, uh, that's really great. Glad he left, and everything seem better for him, at least for you both"

"Yea, thanks, Bev, I appreciate that"

My head hurts just from all the thoughts flooding through my brain and have no idea where Danny is and the one person, I could talk to I was hesitant to tell her the truth or ask questions. I was sobbing indefinitely until I heard a car drive in. I got up quickly and pulled the curtains back and it was Danny, driving in slowly. He turned off the lights and pulled up the handbrake and exit the car and yelled "Liana, Liana, are you awake?"

"Yes, I am Danny, are you okay?"

"Baby I'm sorry about yesterday, I lost my phone, when I realize it was missing I went back to the hospital where I was with Brianna she caught a cold and had an asthma attack so I went to her mom's place and we went there together."

"So why didn't you call me with another phone? You know I would be worried, or even come by my workplace and ask the guards to call me or something? I'm sorry to hear about your daughter, but you had more than enough options to call. Is there something you want to tell me?"

"Liana, are you serious right now? No I don't have anything to tell you apart from what I just

228

mentioned. Let's go inside, please, come on let's go"

I stood there looking at him and trying to process what he had said and thought to myself, why have things changed so drastically? Was that the best story he could create to tell me after being missing for 24 hours?

We went inside, and he was trying hard to convince me where he was, so I asked for the contact number for his ex-wife just to confirm his whereabouts, and he refused. He was furious and kept on yelling that I don't trust him, and will not allow another person to question his character. I wasn't doing that to be honest, I just wanted the truth, I wasn't hoping to get my heart broken again and surely not prepared to be embarrassed at work by everyone who knows our relationship status. I was loss for words, watching him explode for a simple question. My biggest concern now that his voice has an elevated tone was to get him calm and try another approach to eliminate the adrenaline rush and commune to a civil conversation.

"Danny, please calm down; I didn't mean to upset you?" I slowly went towards him and touched him softly, and immediately, I was floating across the room, falling on my side, hitting my face on the television stand. Did Danny just hit me to the ground, I asked myself? But why? My head was spinning, and my body ached, and I looked up at him staring at me, silence and with incredulity.

"Liana, I'm so sorry, I'm so sorry, please forgive me" He hugged me tightly and provided comfort, saying he has extraordinarily strong reflexes and he would never put his hands on me in that manner. Should I believe him? I was hurt, confused and felt abused. He began kissing my tears away, apologizing for his mistake and seemingly intrigued to indulge in a sexual act. I was not in the mood for sex, being in this shocking situation filled with disappointment. But he never seems to think he can be refused at an occasion where sex is not served. He kissed my breast and nipples as I tried to shove him away before he reached my weak spot, letting the curtains open for a fresh start. Before I knew it, I was laying on my back and his warm lips made its way to my love nest, deepening the perfect feeling a girl wants to wake up with in the morning. A relaxed tongue, dripping with saliva, cultivating my clitoris and devouring all my juices. I forgot that I was just smacked in the face and was receptive to his tongue, his kisses and impatient to receive him inside. I wanted to be reluctant but what if he decides to leave me and never to return, I can't lose this great feeling, I want him so bad, I know now he's sorry and it won't happen again; he loves me. The positive thoughts I needed were transparent and allowed my body to react willingly. He punctures my love nest with his desirable manhood, while softening my nipples with his tongue and inserting it deep in my ears making me numb to his touch. Every stroke was replenishing even as I held his waist steadily anticipating a climax, he removed his manhood and rubbed my clitoris vigorously as I distribute my liquefied orgasm towards him. He knew exactly what I wanted as he relaxes my clitoris with his warm tongue another insertion of his manhood developed an increased desire to have us both climax. He was stroking my soft spot and providing consistent comfort to empty my inner weakness on him, watching his shaft diminish strength after the semen was removed.

"Danny", being reluctant as to what to say, he asked that I forgive him for what he did and promised that he will make me happy. "I know you may have times when we'll have disagreements Danny so please don't make promises you cannot keep"

"Let's get you off the floor, okay? he demanded. Are you working today? Maybe you should take the day off, makeup won't be able to cover that scare and I'm sure you wouldn't want our business being exposed at work, right?"

"I'll call my boss Danny" he kissed my forehead and went to the kitchen trying to figure out what to cook for us. "Baby!" he yelled, as I washed my face and turned the shower on, preparing for a bath.

"Yes, Danny," I responded

"What do you want for dinner, chicken or fish?"

"Fish is fine"

"Okay baby fish it is for us then"

I felt sorry for him, he never initiated cooking before, so this was surprising. As much as I am in pain, I felt happy that we had great sex and now he's trying to make up for what he has done. I quickly showered and went to help in the kitchen, but he asked that I relax and watch a movie while dinner is prepared. I called my manager and advised her that I had an accident and is requesting the day off to rest. She was very sympathetic and asked that I take all the time I needed and to contact my team lead to notify her of my absence so that the team's performance is maintained. She was disappointed but advise her it will be only be a few days and to assume leadership until I return.

The look on Danny's face was priceless as he signaled how happy he was that I'm smiling again. Inside, I was hurting but I ignored the feeling and went to hug him from behind. He lifted me up and placed me on the kitchen counter and, poured us both a glass of wine and toasted to a strong lasting relationship. I deserve to be spoiled for a while, yes, eliminating an unhealthy union between us but apart from that I'm now thinking is he the guy for me? I regret having second thoughts, as I noticed his motion of expertise in the kitchen, purifying the atmosphere with aromas of steam fish cooked in coconut milk with broccoli and carrots chopped in large pieces, rice and beans and mash potatoes. He cooked with such passion and grace, allowing me to taste at every stir and occasionally kissing my lips and breast.

I was tempted to ask him about his daughter, but a soft voice asked that I wait and not spoil the moment. I hope she's okay and he won't have to disappear again tonight without saying anything. My mind is disorganized, stifling with fear and curiosity. All I can see when I stared at him is the look on his face when I fell to the ground. What should I do? Should I drive to the beach and relax for a few and clear my head? I think I should call someone, talk to Bev or Peaches to get their perspective, right? The fear of gossiping about what happen dawned on me and I was left just wondering without a concluded answer. I took a deep breath and jumped off the counter and went outside to breathe, relax and think for a minute.

Liana do you want to talk about what happened, Danny asked I was relieve he asked first, and I was ready to listen to his apology yet again and explain what happened so I can move forward.

"Yes Danny, I want you to talk to me this time, not yell, I won't be upset I just want clarity." Calmly he repeated what he had said earlier, and I was satisfied. He went inside the kitchen and set the table for us to have an outside dinner. The food was amazing and tasty. I enjoyed the meal so much I asked for a second plate. He was elated that I gave him a 100% for seasoning the food to perfection - oh yes a man's ego.

FRIENDSHIP UNDER PRESSURE

It was a beautiful evening of laughing and having a good conversation with each other. An unplanned day that was meaningful and relaxing at the same time. Fortunately for him I'm easy to forgive and because of that we were able to have a fruitful evening. I took up the empty plates and pack up the remainder of the food that was on the stove and washed the dishes while he balances his cash for the evening. He was pleased with Robert's work ethics and mentioned he has no regrets hiring him 'yet' then laughed.

"Did you call Peaches, I'm sure she would like to hear the feedback about her man's first day" Danny giggled. I looked for my phone and called immediately to brag about her handy man.

"Peaches, how are things with you darling?'

"I'm great Liana, here waiting on Robert to get home"

"What, he's not home yet?

She was crying but trying hard to hold the tears back. Robert has not been home since last night and she didn't even call me. She is worried that Bobby might be interrogating him and took his phone as she tried calling a few times and the person that answered is not Robert. They were smart and used different names for each other as contact information. Danny called Robert and he answered saying he's home and is doing well, he sounded terrified and indirectly a hint of fear in his voice; maybe it was indication that he was in trouble and needed help. I ran to the bathroom and advise Peaches that she might be in danger if Bobby showed up at Roberts' home so she should try to stay with a friend that Bobby would never think of visiting.

She started packing and after about twenty minutes, Robert called from an unknown number asking us to call Peaches and tell her that he has sent someone there to pick her up and take her to another location, an isolated environment that Bobby doesn't know about, she will be safe there. We acted accordingly and get in touch with Peaches and she was able to confirm that the car was outside. We waited until she got inside the vehicle and speak with the person, which Robert agreed that he's the right guy. How did he escape to call us so quickly, and how did he arrange for a pickup for Peaches so fast? I can't even imagine what just happened.

"Danny asked Robert about what happened with him and Bobby and he explained that when he got off work, he was parked outside and began asking questions about Peaches and why he never came to visit him at the station. He was upset that they are such good friends and he didn't check on him. So he was just punishing him for that. Luckily, no one spilled the beans yet about their relationship, so he was happy about that and decided to take some defensive measures to protect Peaches and the baby. If, and when Bobby finds out, Robert know that he will not be calm and will search the ends of the earth to find her unless he confronts him first. They both agree that now would not be a good time and would allow Bobby some time to settle and regain his sanity before they give him that news.

We were so concerned about Peaches, especially now that Bobby is looking for her, we can't go to the police station since he has not committed a crime. He's only inquiring about her. We just need to ensure she's somewhere remote that he won't search. Danny and I stayed in contact with her until she arrived safely at the destination Robert requested. She was crying and second guessing her decisions and hope that no harm will come to her child when Bobby finds out.

"She will be okay Robert don't worry, if you need anything, please reach out to us and let us know" I reassured him. Danny knew right then and there he would have to get someone else to help him with his workload. Soon after he was finished with his checks and went to shower. I finish cleaning the kitchen and went to lay in bed and wait for him. Thinking back, I feel happy I didn't burden Peaches with my common law affair, she would probably be in the emergency room right now because of all that stress I would burden on her, now that Danny and I have an understanding, I hope this incident doesn't reoccur. He climbed into bed and we cuddled watching a movie on Netflix called 365 days everyone was crazy about, but instead of watching the movie we decided to have one of our own and videotape it – I was out of breath for squirting too much, the bed was soaking wet when we were finished. We spread towels and top of our orgasm and sweat and went to bed.

Danny woke at 6 o'clock and struggled to get to the shower, so I went to the kitchen and made him breakfast and packed some fruits for him to take to work and a protein shake that I'm an expert at making. After he left, I went to the shower and examined the scars and swelling from the previous day and decided to take another day off and use the time to check on Bev. She seems to be doing great with the planning of the wedding and her relationship with Thomas flourishing. I wanted to visit her, but I wouldn't want her to know about what happened, so I stayed home and helped my team lead with the attendance tracker and host a few phone coaching sessions. She was overwhelmed with reports since there was a new promotion and the price reflected on the website was an issue, and the demand for compensation and expectations has increased, so we had to escalate the list of discrepancies to our Manager for an internal fix and to have another team of experts reach out to the customers and offer an alternative that will prevent them from cancelling.

The idea was rewarding as we consistently worked to fix the issue and to avoid continuous escalations we created a call flow script to the agents so they could advise the callers of the error and that we are working aggressively to fix it. We also include that any order that is placed in error will be cancelled and refunded. More so our technical team was advised to upload a message to the site to advise consumers of the error immediately and to prevent orders from being placed since some banks take seven to ten business days to remove an authorization. Our queue was overloaded with calls which led us to recruit a few agents for overtime and if they're not handled the overflow will go to another site that handles the same contract.

Even though I was home I enjoyed the action and hands-on activity at work, the workload, and the opportunity to delegate and see the outcome of my hard work. I felt the fire inside again and want to just get ready and leave for work, I made an attempt to cover the scar with makeup but for persons who knew me very well and is observant will notice a slight difference on my face so I just do what I can from home and helped Meika as much as I could.

CLOSING MOMENTS: REFLECTIONS ON FRIENDSHIP AND LOVE

The day went by amazingly fast a lot of calls about the issues we encountered but the team was able to handle the escalations without frustrations and that was something I was delighted to see happening. They handle each call without hesitation and pose and provide the world-class customer service to the callers as they were thought to do. Even though I was not physically there, I was providing the support they needed, and it was highlighted at the end of the day and appreciated by the team. I was surprised they showed such effort and delicately resolve each situation professionally and displayed such confidence throughout the day to transfer the information correctly to the callers.

My manager called late evening and commended my involvement with the team even though I was out sick. I had promised the team that within two weeks, we will have our pizza day and maybe add more items such as Kentucky Fried Chicken (KFC), snacks, and some candies. Not all the agents prefer Pizza, so we decided to get wings or a bucket of chicken. She had given us some vouchers for Pizza Hut to get a personal pan or at KFC to get a one-piece meal combo. In additional to that she issued a few calling cards to use as an encouragement for agents to complete tasks and reward them with these tokens.

During the call with my manager, Peaches called she was doing better that the day before; she wasn't crying but she sounded unhappy and wanted my opinion about telling Bobby the truth about her and Robert. She thought it would be a good idea since she's pregnant and has been trying for years she would be devastated if she experienced a miscarriage. It may seem insensitive to deny her an answer but, I can't help her make that decision; she would need to consult with Robert what the next step will be.

She was indecisive and wanted my opinion to help make a decision, but I wasn't going to allow anyone to blame me for their mistakes, I'll tell her after that I was thinking of that option. But encourage her to follow her heart and pray about it, and that may help her decide. She deserves a break from feeling unhappy and emotional when problems knock at her door. I am her best friend, yes, but I respects her privacy and want the best for her. She knows I'll always be there for her to support her no matter what happens. She just needs to believe that too.

"Peaches I'll visit you soon okay, I just have to find out where Bobby is at that time, so I know I'm not followed, and I'll be there"

"Sure Liana, I know you will, we just have to be careful right now"

"I'll talk to you later honey"

"Oh Liana, I have good news, Robert went to work this morning so he's okay, thanks to you and Danny for understanding."

"Sure Peaches, it's okay, bye"

Suddenly I heard a car tooting outside, so I ended the call and went to look, and it was Bev. What is she doing her? I thought. I opened the door and waved to acknowledge her to enter. She ran up and hugged me tightly.

"I've missed you. What's up, I heard you are out sick, so I decided to surprise you and I brought you food, your favorite from Kentucky Fried Chicken (KFC), three piece spicy rib, leg and thigh with a corn"

"Oh, you didn't, Bev, thank very much, you know we can share this"

We went inside and I persuaded her to take a bite from the meal she mentioned she is on a diet for her wedding. I'm a bad friend, I know but it was just a small piece of chicken that will not add any pounds, I know it. She was very observant so in my mind, I already create a story to tell her just in case she asks about the scar. Danny and I will be okay, I'm sure, so I'll keep this a secret for now. We talked a lot about work, and she thought I was immensely helpful, delegating on my sick day duties to my team lead at work, when I should be relaxing. One of the topics we never seem to ignore is about

Peaches, we are not gossiping about her, but we are concerned and I told Bev how I really felt, and we began thinking of ways we can help her. Maybe it's best us girls meet with Bobby alone and get his perspective and then move from there or maybe give him the news of the pregnancy and only if he ask who the father is, then we elaborate but meeting Robert with Peaches and then the visibility of a pregnancy he will feel betrayed and in fact think of it as an infidelity since they use to be so close when he was in a relationship with Peaches.

"I think this is a great idea Liana. We just need to decide when to tell her"

"Yea, we just have to find the right day and time to make the suggestion and see what she will do, we know how Peaches is sometimes when it comes on to making a decision, she might disagree and then later hop to it" I added

251

Delighted about the idea, Bev proceeded with her thoughts and final decors for the wedding and what type of food she would like, the final guest list, music and added entertainment. She explained that her invitation will be no more than one hundred and fifty persons. Inclusive of friends and families for Thomas and herself. The menu entails juicy fruit kabobs with a mixture of green and red grapes, ripe red strawberries, sweet juicy pineapples and mangoes and, slightly salted kiwi, grilled spicy and mild deboned chicken breast seasoned to taste kabobs with fried plantains well done, assorted sweet pepper and cucumber, mini burgers with beef and chicken and a variety of sandwiches such as tuna, cheese, ham and vegetable, juices and tea. We were happy to conclude the selection for the cocktail, but ideas about dinner were even more challenging based on religious beliefs, food allergies and personal preferences.

The website for selective menus and choices will be sent to all invited and they will have the opportunity to choose what their intake for dinner will be for the wedding, we will make it clear for all to ensure they choose the foods careful that is aligned with their health and religious views as this will be done to order and no additional amount will be prepared to meet their needs at the wedding. We included the basic that is consumed by most, such as Fish, Chicken, Pork, Beef, Vegan selections and also add an additional preference in the menu listing just in case we have more than ten persons suggesting the same item we may consider adding same and making an exception for those persons. What we would do, however, is contact the person directly and make changes to their order once they agree.

The ideas were defined and ready to be uploaded on the website. She was so elated that she had the chance to finish that task with me and we could decide and laugh together about what we would expect from the guest and their feedback. We made so many jokes and generated some strict rules that will not be changed no matter what happens, this will ensure that the entire list is not rearranged as we all know how group settings can bring confusion when there are suggestions. We may have put in too much work after, more than what we bargain for just because we want the input of the guest and include them a little into the planning. People feel a sense of purpose when they are assigned tasks which will be known to others that they have made a difference. Once there is any sign of complication, the extra support will be removed and the list will remain the same, whereby guests will have to choose from the menu. She has gone over her budget and looking for ways to remove items that are causing too much confusion, or that she seems inconclusive about.

The dresses were on their way and has an estimated delivery date for another two weeks. It's being shipped from the United States from David's Bridal, but one problem leads to another, not a big change but yes she changed the dresses for the bridesmaids from being all-curvy mermaids to an elegant off-the-shoulder chiffon gown accentuating from the bust perfecting each body to its design, capturing an outstanding glow for the bridesmaids' overall appearance. She will, however, own the desire to demonstrate her planned elegant, detailed mermaid dress with intricate, silver designs at the neckline and around the waist on her special day.

"I guess we would look too sexy, huh?" I joked

She was cracking up as we laughed about the change, apparently, I was not updated as I missed the meeting she had with the girls and must have forgotten to asked so when she called me to provide her with the correct measurement, I had no knowledge she made a different decision for the bridesmaids and myself. I wasn't disappointed with the change I think most of the ladies will agree with the gown since it's less revealing and might be more comfortable to wear after a large meal.

She didn't make any changes to the suits for the males so that was great, I guess Thomas would be the one to decide on those changes and to screen the groomsmen to adopt to the change. It's easier most times to make a decision for a male versus a female, for us we can be very overwhelmed when we are uncomfortable with our figure. We may have an issue with our stomach being too obvious in a particular dress or it just doesn't fit right, we may have an over-proportionate breast size that may cause the dress not to fit even though other areas are just perfect. Then we are forced to get an alteration at the tailor or dressmaker to add a finishing touch that provides a satisfactory desire.

"Bev, I hope these dresses are a final decision or this may cause a delay in the alteration upon receipt."

"Don't worry, Liana, I think I have made the right choice and the dresses will be perfect. But in case you are worried I have a tailor reserved to help in that department, so trust me when I say I got you guys"

'Sounds like a plan, I love that Bev, you are so confident and that's what I love. What has Thomas been up to?

"Well I have decided to have lunch with his friend from high school that has recently moved here and has decided last minute that he would like to be invited. I told him the list has been finalized but he insists I have lunch with him and see if I would just invite him for one of our special guests to sing, or do something entertaining at the ceremony or reception."

"Oh, Bev that's good, why not do it, with one condition only if this performance will be for free"

Bev and I laughed so hard we were crying, how silly!

"I would agree with you Liana. Since this is last minute I would be doing him a favor that will cost me extra, unless I can swap him with someone that may change their mind on coming, but for now I haven't had anyone that had decided not to attend."

Well you can meet with him and see what area he will add value to in order to decide what to do. I'm sure we can use him for a special item at the reception. Bev agreed and concluded our conversation. She got up and walked to the door and hugged me. When are you coming back to work? she asked.

I'm hoping tomorrow, Bev, I should be okay by then"

She nodded and walked away towards her car and drove off.

In my mind, I was so nervous around her as my scar was a little visible. I tried hard to have my face opposite towards her so she could not see it. I was so happy she left without noticing.

The following day, Thomas and Bev decided to meet at Tracks and Records on Bottom Road in Montego Bay, a calm and beautiful location and the food there is excitedly tasty so it's one of the number one places to eat and relax in the city. They met Chris on the lawn of the restaurant, which has the statue of the fastest man in the world, a Jamaican athlete, our idol Usain Bolt. We are indefinitely proud to have inherited such a unique talent amongst the additional achievers the island produced.

Since Thomas was new in town, we took a few pictures in front of the statue where Usain Bolt posed with his famous lightning bolt pose which symbolizes his legendary alethic skills. Shortly after we then proceeded to our reservation, which was located to the upper part of the building, viewing the unconditional beauty of the city entertained with tourist and the abundance of gift shops sharing the island's sentimental culture. The ambiance and staff were amazing, the colors painted inside the beautiful setting represent the Jamaican flag, black, green and gold, the spectacular design was aligned closely to our own ancestral tradition assimilated with professionalism and island vibe.

Chris has a warm and friendly personality and seems to be a very good conversationalist, providing us with great ideas we could include on the invitation to entertain our guests. A conversation that was fully enjoyed until our food was ready. He had so many ideas about the wedding and stage performances that were valid which Thomas and I agreed on firstly. They were thoughts we had shared with each other but decided to change and have entertainment that are traditional. We are were laughing at every idea and it felt good. Seeing Thomas so enthused and filled with excitement was stifled for months, but I thought it was the stress of planning the wedding. He needed more of this time out with friends to relax and laugh. I listened and tried to memorize the ideas as the heat of the moment after this deliciousness will scramble my thoughts and restrict me from having a clear memory, so I quickly took out my pocketbook and wrote all we have discussed. Once the waiter cleared the table, they took the bill, and Chris decided to pay it all.

"Chris, I appreciate that, but I would like for us to split the bill?" I suggested

"No, no, no Bev, it would be my pleasure to take care of the bill for us, please it's fine" Chris insisted "Babe, it's okay, Chris thank you we'll tip the waiter instead," Thomas added "Guys it's fine, I promise I'll take care of it all" Chris demanded We kept quiet and allowed him do take care of the bill, however what surprises me the most is seeing the amount he paid for tip. It was a very generous amount but who am I to judge. I totally would rate the services provided by the restaurant and staff as excellent, it was worth the time.

We left the dining area and went to the bar, enjoying a few shots of tequila and Crown Royal on the rocks before we went our separate ways. For a moment, we were lost in the melody of the famous Reggae legend Bob Marley's soothing vocals, capturing my mind and body as we all gesticulated in moments of reggae tonic movements.

Thomas looked at me and smiled and asked my decision with Chris coming to the wedding and excitedly, I agreed, "he's officially a special guest Thomas" I giggled.

We all had our last drink and said our goodbyes while standing at Chris car, which was parked closer, and Thomas and I walked to ours as we giggled and laugh about what will happen next. It was an exciting evening of warm souls tending to each personality and having a good time, something I desperately needed for Thomas and I. We haven't had the chance to enjoy each other but today was a gift. A moment we needed before the wedding just to relax with a friend.

It was like Déjà vu as he opened the door for me and we glanced at each other, remembering an evening like this before and yes, I got the signal. Driving home, I decided to tease him a little, so we set the mood with some soothing love songs, moving our bodies to each rhythm as the fresh air entered our lungs as we yelled in happiness. I pushed my seat back and placed my hands under my dress, trying to entertain him while driving, spreading my legs and inserting my fingers in my love nest and tasting myself with deep seduction as the slime of my orgasm lingers from my lips, leaving small drops of fluids on my breast, demanding the feeling of desires with the warmth of his tongue and solid shaft entering mi Dulce Tierra with passion.

The clock was ticking, and the obvious bulge of his manhood stretched to visibility, earning the opportunity to exit the zipped entranced. My mouth was already warm and ready to make my lips fit perfectly over his pink-headed, well-erected, veined, attractive organ, testing my skills at the very top, increasing his sensation and hoped he would concentrate and take us home safely. I took him all in loudly making strokes with saliva and constant deep throats just to hear him moan and hold my head when I consumed him all as he yelled my name in silence.

"Don't stop, baby. You know exactly what I want?" Thomas whispered.

I was on my knees on the passenger side, deepening my strokes as he used his left hand to grip my evenly paired ass, inserting his thumb slightly at the entrance activating my sex drive into full speed. He was desperate and pulled in our driveway as he pulled his seat back, giving me adequate space to climb on top, feeling the contraction of mi gatita on his polla.

Touching my g-spot and opening the portal of orgasms, making each stroke easier and deeper. Suddenly he pushed me upwards and held me close, as he speeds with anxiousness, deepening his thrust inside my love nest, gripping my hair and kissing my lips with love. I then find myself on my knees with half my body on the passenger side and spreading my butt cheeks as he continuously pounded her increasingly fast and used his thumb to play with mi culo sending shivering feels of ecstasy to every nerve in my body, desperate to climax. The sound of our moans, united in harmony keeping his hands busy as he spanked my cheeks as his excitement to climax draws near.

"Fuck, I'm coming baby, fuck Bev, baby this pussy is mine forever, Ohhh, fuck, Yes!" Thomas yelled as drops of his warm sperm splashed across my ass and back.

Trying to catch my breath, we looked at each other and smiled as I sat with my legs on the dashboard, trying to see through the frost we made on the window. Thinking like a child, I used my index finger to make a heart on the window and stared at him, gesturing a smile. We got dressed and went inside the house, and not before long we cuddled and went to bed with our bodies as one. I woke up at about 3am and, went to the bathroom, and kept on smiling about how happy I'd be in a couple of months when I said "I do", marrying the man of my dreams. I can't ask for anything more - this is the happiness I was waiting for. I washed my hands and went back to bed, cuddling his warm body as I listened to him snore. Within minutes, the sound put me to sleep.

GLOSSARY

mi dulce tierra - my sweet land

Mi culo - my Ass

mi gatita - my love nest

polla - Cock / Penis

www.ingramcontent.com/pod-product-compliance
Lightning Source LLC
Chambersburg PA
CBHW070913120626
46546CB00001B/248